CRIES FROM A
Metis Heart

LORRAINE MAYER

CRIES FROM A
Metis
Heart

By Lorraine Mayer

PEMMICAN
PUBLICATIONS
INC.

Pemmican Publications gratefully acknowledges the assistance accorded to its publishing program by the Manitoba Arts Council, the Province of Manitoba – Department of Culture, Heritage and Tourism, Canada Council for the Arts and Canadian Heritage – Book Publishing Industry Development Program.

Printed and Bound in Canada
First Printing: 2007

Library and Archives Canada Cataloguing in Publication

Mayer, Lorraine, 1953-
    Cries from a Métis Heart/written by Lorraine Mayer
Includes poems.
Includes bibliographical references.

ISBN: 978-1-894717-43-4

    1. Mayer, Lorraine, 1953-. 2. Métis. 3. Métis women-Biography. 4. Métis-Biography. I. Title

FC109.1.M39A3 2007   971.004'970092   C2007-904248-1

PEMMICAN PUBLICATIONS INC.
Committed to the promotion of Metis culture and heritage
150 Henry Ave., Winnipeg, Manitoba, R3B 0J7, Canada
www.pemmican.mb.ca

 Canada Council   Conseil des Arts
for the Arts   du Canada

 Canadian   Patrimoine
Heritage   canadien

 MANITOBA arts COUNCIL
CONSEIL DES arts DU MANITOBA

 Manitoba

I would like to dedicate this book to the memory of my mother, Dora Mayer, along with my daughter, Danielle, and granddaughters, Ashley, Kianna and Emma.

Acknowledgment

This work owes its life to more than a single author or idea. It is the culmination of a lot of people believing in the need to have the story told. Because this story comes from the heart of a Metis woman it was important to me that a Metis publishing company accept the manuscript, and I was not disappointed. I would like to thank Pemmican Publications for taking a risk with this project. In particular, I thank my editor Randal McIlroy for his patience, absolute faith in the project and his ability to guide me past panic and into completion. It has been more than a pleasure to travel the last steps of this particular journey with Randal. To my dear friend Sandra Tomsons who willingly spent hours reviewing my manuscript amid shared laughter, tears and many cross-cultural challenges I say thank you. I also want to thank Sandra for seeing the philosophy crafted in the narrative. I would also like to thank Di Brandt for her early reading of my poems and the wonderful technical guidance she provided. I would also like to thank Tomson Highway for showing me time to laugh. I will be eternally grateful for the inspiration, strength and belief I received from the late Dr. R. Robert C. Proudfoot. I would not have come to this point without his belief in the narrative.

Words cannot express the love and gratitude I feel for my family, I honour the sacrifices, the beliefs and hopes of my children and grandchildren. I also want to acknowledge my brothers and sisters for the life we share, and to thank them for loving me through the hard times. The courage to confront my legacy I owe to my mother; to her memory, I hold myself and this book accountable.

Table Of Contents

Foreword
By Sandra Tomsons

The story between the pages of this book is more than a cry from the heart of one Metis woman; it is celebration of victory over oppressions and victimization. Lorraine Mayer, in poetry and prose, allows us into her heart, mind and spirit and also into the spirit and philosophy of the Metis nation. She takes us on her journey through childhood abuse and violence in her family and the terror of spousal abuse it spawned. We watch her spirit unfold as the child, who vowed not to hide in back alleys or to cover her brown Metis skin, grows into a woman dedicated to ensuring her grandchildren can dream.

Lorraine tells us two stories. While relating her personal struggles and triumph, she recounts the story of Metis dispossession and colonization. As Lorraine moves painfully, slowly and fully into her Metis identity, accepting the two nations that birthed her, she discovers the means to self-worth and healing she had sought for a lifetime. And she discovers her warrior voice – her contribution to healing the Metis nation.

The parallel between the domination Lorraine lives as a child and wife and the domination the Metis nation lives in its relationship with Canada is as compelling as it is shocking. The book speaks to those who have been sexually abused and devalued and marginalized by racism. It offers hope that comes from first understanding 'I am not to blame', and then, 'I can still become fully me.' Lorraine rages at the sources of abuse. Not relieving individuals of their share of responsibility, she demonstrates that the fundamental cause of the abuse she, her family and her people suffer is colonialism. The beliefs, attitudes and attendant actions and policies of the Canadian state, which unjustly dispossessed and continues to illegitimately rule the Metis people, have eaten away at the Metis heart, mind and spirit. The weakened community produces weak individuals. Like Lorraine, who overcame the forces trying to destroy her pride and power, and ultimately her being, the Metis too can withstand. Oppression does not have to be victorious. Reconnection to the source of energy for the spirit of the individual and the nation provides the means to victory.

Lorraine shows us in her powerful biography and philosophical exploration of her life and Metis history that personal and community power and healing have their roots in the love and teachings of the grandmothers. These do not erase the huge problems facing a Metis person and the Metis nation; they do enable one to hold onto oneself and enable the Metis community to maintain its integrity.

I am a non-Aboriginal woman, a Eurocentric philosopher. My main research area is Aboriginal rights, particularly in Canada. For me, and I suspect non-Aboriginal readers generally, one of the most insightful aspects of this book is its vivid portrayal of the emotional and cognitive dissonance of Metis experience. The common choice for a Metis person, which is to live as either French or Cree, means one rejects a part of oneself. Personal despair and family conflict attach to either choice. Lorraine's early choice was her Cree heritage.

I think that it is primarily as a Cree woman that Lorraine experiences the world. She knows the philosophy of her French ancestry – its beliefs about knowing the world, what is real and how to live. However, it is Cree ways of knowing, Cree understanding of reality and Cree understanding of being in relationships that constitute her way of seeing and being in the world. In **My Metaphysical Reality** she shows us that her chosen worldview is neither understood nor respected by Eurocentric philosophers. At best, these scholars judge her philosophy to be less than knowledge; at worst, it is not real philosophy but merely superstition. Non-Aboriginal people necessarily and unconsciously experience the world through a conceptual framework that creates obstacles to understanding and respecting Lorraine's wisdom. However, I see in her penetrating prose and poetry the power to help her reader overcome Western philosophy's presumed superiority. One by one the barriers to respecting her philosophy fall as non-Aboriginal readers begin to see the world through her eyes.

In "Binding the Sash" there is some suggestion that healing for Lorraine and for the Metis nation involves becoming one. The individual and the nation must accept being Aboriginal and non-Aboriginal – must identify as Metis. In the poem "We are Both" she expresses the reality of the choices that racism wrought; but, she argues it is impossible that a Metis person is only half a self.

"Me Indian
You white
As if we could just be one
And not the other
With a French dad
And "half-breed" mother

We are both
We are Metis"

Lorraine has to stop rejecting one part of herself to be fully healed. Without this wholeness, she will remain fractured and her spirit limited. Her healing requires reconciling the two philosophies that birthed her. When Metis individuals become whole, no longer split themselves in two, and no longer deny and condemn a part of themselves, then the Metis community will be a free Metis nation.

In the **Binding the Sash** section, Lorraine forcefully attacks the uninformed and unsubstantiated views of political theorist and advisor of politicians, Thomas Flanagan. He argues that the differences between Indian tribes and European nations, and between Indian way of life and European way of life, prove European superiority. Lorraine responds by insisting that her Indian "blood" provides a portion of her beauty. Confident in the value of her Creeness, she calls the actions that made Metis homeless piracy. The purportedly 'civilized' European nations are really lawless, greedy exploiters.

Lorraine informs us that as Europeans call some plants weeds and want to eliminate them, so they viewed the Metis as inferior. Consequently, thoughtlessly and without guilt they uprooted 'Metis weeds' to make room for more valuable 'settler plants.' In "The Fiddler Man" Metis dispossession is expressed in the sadness of the fiddler playing to the loss of his community, Ste. Madeleine

"Cleared of Metis
Cleared for cows."

Repeatedly trampled, the Metis heart has nonetheless resisted destruction and assimilation. The Metis have survived, and as Lorraine repeats in "Red Weeds," the Metis are free. However, as revealed in other portions of her book, Metis freedom is not yet *fully* realized. It can only be partially realized by individuals or communities so long as Canada remains a colonial state.

In the final section of the book Lorraine examines the power and powerlessness of philosophy. A student of European philosophy, she knows the prominent place it accords justice, and she pointedly asks: "Where is justice for her Metis nation?" Those upholding the value of justice steal Metis land and deny Metis values. When she challenges their notions of justice she is told, "be fair." She rightly insists that Socrates, widely regarded as the father of Western philosophy, did not intend such hypocrisy to be the foundation for justice.

Lorraine reveals the many-sidedness of Eurocentric philosophy's hypocrisy. Defining itself as the love of and search for truth, it arrogantly assumes that none is to be found in Aboriginal worldviews. The term 'philosophy' it reserves for its wisdom. She correctly charges contemporary philosophy as being "The Love of Western Wisdom." Also, she is right that only when Western philosophy appropriates 'the wisdoms' of other peoples so that they *become* Western philosophy are the wisdoms real wisdom. Western appropriation transforms what was superstition or dogma into knowledge.

Lorraine, a philosopher who is both inside and outside the Western philosophical tradition, is well positioned to critique its assumed superiority and the narrowness of its search for truth. Despite the academy's devaluing of her and her philosophy, Lorraine discovered more than the depths of her anger as she worked her way to a PhD. She found an outlet for her warrior courage and the means to make a space for her wisdom. The strong voice with which she explained colonialism's multiple injustices and the clarity with which she explained the Metis way of being in the world would allow her grandchildren to live *their* philosophy. Her dream is that they live Metis freedom, not the Canadian oppression that aims to destroy Metis spirit.

Through the power of her poetry and prose, Lorraine brings her reader into her life and into the history of the Metis nation. I have not been unaware of my white-woman-middle-class privileges. However, by bringing me into her personal experience, Lorraine supplies an emotive content that enriches my understanding. This passion, which I identify with the sense of justice Socrates claims is naturally in the human soul, brings me into relationship and into awareness of responsibility. By bringing me into the experience of the Metis nation, Lorraine confronts me with the racism embedded in Western experiencing of the world. She shows me how distorted ways of seeing have produced and sustain the colonial relationship. Again, the response is a sense of injustice. In this context, I am able to see the specifics of non-Aboriginal responsibility in the relationship. Lorraine enlists me, a mother and a philosopher specializing in social and political philosophy, in helping create a Metis future for her grandchildren. This undertaking is not selfless. Only a Metis future contains an honorable future for my grandchidren – a future in which my grandchildren are not oppressing hers. When respect flows in both directions, then the justice of European philosophy and the harmony of Metis philosophy create and sustain the peace and friendship between peoples that Lorraine and I have in our relationship with one another.

Cries From A Metis Heart

Sandra Tomsons earned her PhD in philosophy from Queen's University. Her area of specialization is social and political philosophy, and for more than a decade she has made Aboriginal rights and environmental ethics her major research areas. Lorraine Mayer has been her teacher in the area of Native Philosophy since 1997. They organized an international conference on Philosophy and Aboriginal rights for the Canadian Philosophical Association in 2001.

Introduction

REFLECTIONS

My constant companion
is the gloom of the room
where I chose to sit.
Yet each time I know
the room will draw
me to depths
of aloneness.
And I wonder how
a room so innocent
can bring forth such
intensity of despair
as if it permeates from
the very walls.
I ponder my sense of
alienation . . . knowing
others, even friends
can see my clothes,
my hair
then make assumptions
about me
about who I am.
But
none have ever known me
no, none ever did.
My solitary room
gives another injection
of loneliness that
penetrates my flesh
and the tears fall . . . so

I leave the room with its
intoxicating loneliness
and seek out a friend's
advice on how to ease my pain.
"Survival" he says
"It's merely a sign of your
survival don't you see?
Your feelings brought to life.
The tears, the overwhelming
feelings it's all OK.
It's all about survival."
"It hurts too damn much,"
I say.
My friend laughs
a hollow sound
that offers no warmth.
"It means you're human,"
he says.
"It's human to feel
the pain that crushes
your very being."
And now my friend
you say
"Get mad.
Let it out.
Let it out.
You know you can.
You know you must.
It will destroy you
if you don't."
If I cry I am human?
If I get mad will I survive?
When can I laugh and
be human?
When can I simply smile
and be human?
When can I survive
without the incessant

flow of tears or rage?
When goddammit, when?
"When you let it out,"
he says.
"What is it?" I ask
"What is it I have to let out?"
"Your history, my friend.
Your history"

Intellectually I understood the need to examine my history. I knew the effects of colonialism had left a scar that was continuing to plague my family, but on an emotional level I did not fully comprehend what that history entailed. Before I wrote the above poem I had never realized how important confronting my history would be, to me, to my family and to other Aboriginal women. You see, it is not just my history that needed confronting; it was the history of every Aboriginal woman from 1492 through to 2006. I am talking about confronting the history of violence that followed on the heels of European advancement. It was a legacy of domination and abuse that like a wildfire has run unchecked throughout the Aboriginal women's history. Unfortunately unlike a wildfire, violence has not run its course. "Colonization in and of itself is a violent process. It brought many untold forms of violence against the women, children and men of the Americas."[1]

When the Europeans first came to this continent they sought out Aboriginal women for companionship, survival and simply as a means to gain economic trade relations with different Native communities. Nonetheless, the women in of themselves were not valued beyond what they could do for the European. Early abuses were rampant, from physical to spiritual to emotional abuse. Far too often men would take wives, spawn offspring and then cast the Indian women off at will. Eventually the mixed blood women replaced the Native women. Then as white women began to arrive the mixed blood was also dismissed. These women were used as chattel, beasts of burden and sex slaves described with the derogatory term, "squaw." This tendency is still seen in the treatment of Aboriginal women today.

In Canada today, Aboriginal women aged 25 through to 44 are five times more likely to die of violence than any other Canadian woman of the same age. More than 500 Aboriginal women have gone missing or been murdered over the last 30 years.[2] With such glaring statistics it is safe to say Aboriginal women are living in constant danger, a danger that arose with the treatment and negative stereotypes that began centuries ago. The danger to our lives is so incessant that one of my students once wrote, "By being a Native women it is like there is a dark cloud over your head; you feel like you are just waiting – waiting for your turn to be the next victim. You are waiting to become a statistic but trying your hardest to be one of the positive stats."[3]

It is a disgrace to Canada that Aboriginal women wait out their lives wondering if and when they will be assaulted. Helen Betty Osborne was one such woman who became a statistic. She was killed in 1971 at The Pas, Man. and it took 17 years before any charges were laid. Even with the case finally reaching the courts, justice was not completely served; only one of the four men involved in her death was charged. Many more cases have not been heard, and Aboriginal women continue to suffer as can be seen in the Stolen Sisters phenomenon. The case of the Highway of Tears is a glaring example of how little the Aboriginal woman is valued. Many Aboriginal women went missing along Highway 16 between Prince George and Prince Rupert.[4] However, it wasn't until a white woman went missing along this highway that something was done. If that is not bad enough, there are also instances where Aboriginal women have called the police for help only to be ignored until it is too late to save them. The case with Doreen Leclair and Corrine McKeown, two Metis sisters, is a prime example. The tragic deaths of these two Aboriginal women in Winnipeg should have been avoided considering they made five 911 calls to the Winnipeg police and eight hours later were found stabbed to death.[5] One of my students made a similar call to the police for help – a call that was ignored. Later, a non-Aboriginal man called the police and they responded to his call immediately. It is interesting and quite revealing that the second call was not to help the Aboriginal woman, but a response to the caller claiming that a Native woman was chasing a white man.

Knowledge of these types of racist attitudes has not escaped the notice of Aboriginal women, and it significantly affects how we perceive our safety, value and sense of self. It is obvious that Aboriginal women continue to suffer horrendous abuse not only from people outside their culture but also from within. While we may understand where the abuse originated it does not make the suffering less intense or more acceptable. For example, scholars make clear that, "Today, we are faced with epidemic, lateral violence in our communities. State and church policies started this vicious cycle by instilling violence in children who were placed in residential schools and abusive foster homes, and by degrading women sexually, politically and socially."[6]

Every Aboriginal woman I have ever talked to has mentioned some form of abuse, be it sexual, physical or mental. In one study done in 1989, the Ontario Native Women's Association found that eight out of 10 Aboriginal women were abused. On a daily basis I hear horror stories from my students, so I know these statistics are not decreasing. The Government of Canada is working toward polices directed toward helping "at-risk" populations. In terms of policies, they are looking at the socio-economic conditions such as poor health programs, poor housing, single parenting and so forth, but given the statistics on violence it clear that Aboriginal women were and still are "at-risk" populations simply because of their brown skin. Statistics serve many purposes, not the least of which is informing the general public of the truth of our situations and hopefully force the necessary changes. I have no argument with the need for policy changes, but I want to go beyond policy to show the perceptual reality we as Aboriginal women live with on a daily basis. I cannot tolerate injustice, and everywhere around me I see injustice. The words, "Drunken Indian, Dirty Squaw, Easy and Lazy" are not going away. They are so firmly embedded in the minds of Canadians that "even Native people have, in dark times, internalized these beliefs about their grandmothers, their aunties, their daughters, and themselves."[7] I have lived in my own dark times and responded as such.

I wrote the poem that opened this introduction when I realized that what I had kept hidden for so long was the very thing that was destroying me — secrets — history — denial. It is the same secrecy that hides behind too many Aboriginal women's faces. The following poems and story were written in order to cofront and deal with the secrets, my/our history and the denial that prevented me from living a full life. These secrets allowed me to continue to degrade myself by blaming my actions and inactions on the fact of my birth. Without realizing it, I had bought into the myths created about Aboriginal women. I saw, felt and believed that I was a worthless half-breed. This belief has impacted all my life through my actions and inactions. Until I began to grasp my history, however, I knew none of this.

I had spent much of my life in silence yet found a way to speak and that was in writing poetry. When I could not share my feelings I simply wrote them out. I had never intended to write a book. I merely wanted to ease my pain in secrecy.

Life has a funny way of unfolding, and part of that unfolding for me became this book. I am a Metis woman who has suffered cultural abuse; a mother who has experienced tremendous physical, emotional and spiritual abuse; and I am a grandmother who does not want to see this legacy passed onto her grandchildren. I am the child of a half-breed woman from The Pas, Man. and a French man from Fisher Branch, Man. Along with my parents our home was filled with 10 children. Later in life I learned how country adoption had also impacted whom we called brother, sister and cousin.[8] One has to wonder what such knowledge does to a child's sense of security and trust and identity.

I was the last child born up north at The Pas. I lived most of my youth in Winnipeg, however, returning to the north as an adult and eventually running away from my family and staying away for 22 years. Why did I run? I was trying to escape the violence and the craziness that was a never-ending part of our family existence.

I returned home in July of 2004 after receiving a PhD in Philosophy. I thought that if I came home with this accomplishment my brothers and sisters would finally love me, want me and respect me. While they may have loved me prior to my running away I had other perceptions of how they felt, and it was my perceptions that guided my life.

Being reunited with my family has been an amazing journey. We are coming to know each other again. It is sometimes hard because we have grown and experienced so much, without being near enough to share the experiences, that we are like strangers. Even though we now range from 30s to 60s, sometimes we treat each other like we had when we were children. Yet that is normal – maybe the only normal thing we've ever done.

This book is about how my life unfolded, and as such it is filled with pain, but it is not just about pain. This book is also about recovery; it is about facing the unknown. So, while it is about injustice, family injustice, cultural injustice and personal injustice, it is more importantly about refusing to keep silent. My mother, so concerned with what others would think, taught me a philosophy of silence, but I no longer hold to her philosophy of "don't tell" or "what will people think." For my sanity I found I must fearlessly confront the past, including my own choices. This book is a testament to my recovery and all the pain, guilt and humiliation that have followed me throughout my life. It is also a book about pride – pride in my womanhood and in my Metis identity, my Metis history and the complicity that envelops Metis people as we struggle to make sense of the world that rejects us, ridicules us and denies us. So while I call this a book about my life it is also a book about other Metis women. In fact it is a book that speaks to many women's experiences, since many Metis women have suffered from historical trauma and like myself struggle to overcome the most debilitating destruction. Somehow we have to give ourselves permission not only to live but also to thrive. This is particularly difficult for those of us women to whom everything including our own thought processes takes on the appearance of a threat. For myself I eventually came to realize that by locking my experiences deep with myself and never sharing them I was allowing the shame and humiliation of my experiences to live, festering, eating away at me daily, destroying my ability to function in the world as fully human with dignity. My writing that began in secret has become the key to unlocking my self-imposed prison and to eventual freedom.

While writing I came to a place where I wondered what my grandmother, if she were alive, would have thought of her granddaughter, and so I asked her in the only way I knew how:

GRANDMOTHER
Grandmother where are you
I hear you calling but I hurt
Grandmother
am I the woman you thought
the child would be?
No!
Beer, wine and men
took the place of beads, hide and pride

Grandmother I hear you calling
but I am ashamed of who I am
Grandmother keep calling
I'm coming home
Grandmother – I am
Yes!
Wait for me grandmother
I'm coming home.

I talk to my grandmother. I wish I knew her. I wish I knew my mother better than I did. I began to understand that their history is not unlike mine. I am sure the circumstances were different, but the feelings would have been the same. When I was younger I did not have the appreciation for my mother that I should have had; in fact I blamed her for marrying my white father and making me a mixed blood. I blamed her for not being like the perfect moms I found in storybook novels, or moms who went to PTA meetings instead of Bingo. Indeed, there is not much I didn't try to blame her for even as I found myself growing into her:

Lorraine Mayer

WOMAN STILL CHILD

Where does she go
a woman still child
To whom does she turn?
when no one's around
the woman still child
expected to live
to dry her own tears
to have strength never learned
expected to be woman

Where does she go
a woman still child?
From whom does she learn
a nurturing love
the safety in trust
expected to know
how to cuddle and laugh
to cherish her child
expected to be mother

Where does she go
A woman still child
birthed
from a woman still child,
Birthed from a woman
still child
A legacy of emptiness
expected to know
they were women
when their heritage
was stolen.

So much has been taken from us Metis women, indeed from all women. I was particularly struck by our silence one day when Vanda Fleury, a Metis student, said that she was happy I was writing because too many women hold the same fears, hurts and humiliations yet live every day feeling terribly alone. For Vanda and every other woman who has suffered in silence I hope the words I have written ease your pain and strengthen you by knowing you are not alone and that what others may call dysfunction may in fact be survival skills, for they have allowed many of us to survive amid constant onslaughts to our identity and our very being.

NOTES

[1] Kim Anderson. A Recognition of Being: Reconstructing Native Womanhood. Toronto: Second Story Press, 2000, p.97.

[2] Joyce Green. "Missing Women" Canadian Dimension, 2004.

[3] This statement was taken from an unpublished paper written by Christa Templeton. Brandon University, April 12, 2006.

[4] Anna Hunter. "The Violence that Indigenous Women Face" Canadian Dimension, 2005.

[5] Bryan D. Cummins & John L. Steckley. Aboriginal Policing: A Canadian Perspective. Toronto: Prentice Hall, 2003, pp. 83-84.

[6] Anderson, 2000, p. 97

[7] Anderson, 2000, p. 99.

[8] Country adoption involved a non-legal but culturally accepted way of taking into one's home another family member's child and raising that child as one's own. While the tendency to provide a home is admirable, the secrecy surrounding parentage that followed some of these country adoptions created confusion and hurt over who was truly one's brother or sister or who were in fact one's parents.

Ambivalence

1

"**I** don't know why my brothers keep marrying these half-breed women!" These words have haunted my memory for many years and I wonder whether my aunty realized that we knew her love came with deceit. I lived with tremendous deceit all my life and often the only way to survive was to write out my pain. And so I write to tell you who I am. The story of my life reveals the ambivalence I felt from both within and outside my family circle. It is not fun being a mixed blood child, and while scholars debate the implausibility of race, one simple fact remains: the births resulting from the union of two distinct nations, whether harmonious or through enforced rape, have often resulted in racist and discriminatory attitudes within one's own family. Innocent children are hurt and these children grow into adulthood quite often struggling to make sense of their identities.

Mixed bloods in Canada are conceptualized in a slightly different way from those in other countries. In the United States or South America, identification as a mixed blood culminates in the forced rejection of one bloodline. This is especially true for people of black pigmentation; consider how the one-drop rule in the United States[9] forces black identity while in Canada the whole damn bucket is needed for Indian identity.[10] We can argue endlessly and reject theories of racial difference, we can create new and newer theories to explain cultural differences, yet children are still being hurt. Take the Metis child's history, for many mixed blood children rejection of one bloodline is often a self-imposed rejection.

We can glamorize the history of Louis Riel, we can parade the Metis accomplishments in the fur trade, we can acknowledge the difference between ourselves and the First Nations or ourselves and the White Nations. We can brag with pride about our heritage. We are not either/or – we are both. But, can we distance ourselves far enough from the pain of the cultural conflicts that give rise to our existence and the lived reality of disillusionment that stems from interfamily interactions? We can bury it in the deepest recess of our minds, but it surfaces over and over again to remind us that we act out who people say we are. Arturo Aldama, a mestizo scholar, says he learned at an early age to "negotiate contradictions."[11] It is these negotiations and contradictions that I am concerned with and where they took me on my life's journey.

Sometimes the process of negotiating is fraught with intense self-dislike, other times it is fraught with rage at others. In both cases it quickly leads to a sense of alienation. I felt this sense of alienation far too often. In the midst of one particular mind-divorcing alienation I wrote my rage at my father; for what I am no longer sure. At the time I only knew I had to get the rage out of my system; I had to or it could kill me. So I wrote:

DANCING THROUGH THE FOG
You poor white trash working class man
spawning mixed blood light-brown child
I guess you didn't know any better
I guess you thought you loved her

Did her sparkling deep-brown eyes draw
you into depths your own denied you?
Enticing seductress, spinning webs
your family called her *half-breed*.

An unwanted, unfit bride
with skin so brown she did her best
to hide with creamy cakes of white.
Is this what made her beautiful?

You poor white trash working class man
did drink make her more acceptable
as you danced her through the fog
till her spirit died?

My mother lived her life knowing her in-laws, well at least some of them, saw her as less than valuable. My mother was beautiful yet I would watch her carefully spread white makeup all over her face before she would leave our home, and I vowed never to cover my face, no matter how brown the sun would paint me.

I think back to how my mother would walk down back allies carrying parcels full of groceries and realized that my aunt was not alone in her arrogance and contempt for half-breeds. So were our neighbours, and my mother knew it. I vowed never to walk down back allies. I would march down main walkways with my head held high. Oh yes, I could make these vows all I wanted, but when it came down

Cries From A Metis Heart

to it, I copied my mother's patterns of protection. Too often she hid from prying eyes and her favourite words were, "what will the neighbours say." She taught her children to live the philosophy of denial. We learned to hide what happened in our house. We learned to hide who we were, what we ate and how we felt.

I think often about my aunt's thoughtless, racist words, echoing in a room where innocent children began to carry the scars of her malignant poison. I may not have covered my skin with white makeup, but I always felt rejected by her and every other "white" woman, man and child. So when I read theories that talk about how we internalize oppression I find myself in turmoil. Yes, there is the oppression from within and from outside, but what about for those of us who come from both outside and inside? Where do we go? Who do we turn to? Where does it end? When does it end, this feeling of aloneness?

No child should have to feel the intensity of racial and family bigotry or need to disassociate from herself in order to survive. Yet, I felt disassociated, compartmentalized and objectified from a very young age. I have lived behind a veil of ignorance in many ways, always searching for connection to myself. I would long for a time when I could feel; I mean really feel . . . love. And while scholars write incessantly about oppression, "autocolonialism,"[12] I hear my history in every song, in every story, in every poem:[13]

FORGOTTEN CHILD
Wandering lost
in a mist of pain
forgotten child
without her land
echoes of thundering
hooves pounding
in her head
visions of buffalo
dust choking
off her breath
excitement coursing
in her veins
running free
with the land
...
jolted back
to a barrenness

no buffalo
no dust
no one
forgotten child
weeps alone
who will dry her tears?
Lost without land
floating from home
to home
hiding in shadows
afraid to be seen.
Trembling soul
of forgotten child
who will dry her tears
who will love her
who will want her
forgotten Indian child

But in truth I am not an Indian child. Yet I chose years ago to identify with the part of me that loved me, my mother's family. I loved the bush, the bannock, the laughter that flowed so freely up North. I loved the sound of Cree, the teasing and the laughter. I felt my mother's safety when we were up North and I felt her fear in the city, so I chose to be Native with a heart for the north. I came to despise my white side and the city.

Cross-racial adoption may benefit some people, but for others it is destructive. While denying one side of our ancestry gives some comfort it nonetheless robs us of our full cultural self and identity. It is not so much that rejection of one side of one's ancestry is necessary or the best thing to do, but rather that we heal the legacy of abuse that has haunted and destroyed so many of our families. Too many children are raised without value or come into an adult world where they are dismissed, as was my mother. I raged at the injustice to her, to me, and so I wrote:

RAGING BLOODY MURDEROUS RAGE
Raging bloody murderous rage
erupting from innocent veins
spreading pungent poison – rape
across this filthy land.

You in your cocksure arrogance
dragging red roots from their soil
choking out the mystery of our life

The terror of my memory pounding
on my drum beat
scarcely echoes in your hearts.
Everywhere I see the whiteness of my death
ripping through a virgin womb
while greed hooks drag my history through
your soiled forgotten past.

But wait, your past is living
in my time and I a bitch
a slut a whore
raped beaten, used abused.
with haunted daytime dreams
survives this bloody murderous rage.
Fuck you I won't go down.

Fuck you . . . fuck you
Fuck you.

Oh yes, there was pain in my childhood, just as there is pain in many, many
mixed blood children's homes. And while I am aware that not all families suffer,
mine did. The above poem was written to expel the rage that I knew came from
my own ancestry.

I once wrote:
I come from a culture of genocide
I come from a culture of pride . . .

Who am I angry with? My white side or my Indian side? Ironically,
scholars argue that racial identities are a social construction and not based on any
scientific reality. I wish my life was just a figment of someone's imagination; maybe
then I could escape the reality of the pain that has been inflicted, or maybe I could
pretend that my pain, like my race, is also a figment of someone's imagination.[14]

My white side or my Indian side, since as Spencer and Naomi Zack say,
both sides are a figment of someone else's construction. I wish my life was
just a figment; maybe then I could escape the reality of the pain that has been

inflicted, or maybe I could pretend that my pain, like my race, is also a figment of someone's imagination.

There is so much to overcome when you are born into a world that is still divisionary, racist and oppressive. The strength to survive and to identify with one particular culture is not as much a matter of perpetuating racial division as much as it is of saving oneself from the intense pain of cognitive dissonance. What is cognitive dissonance after all if not the internal pain of confusion, of finding ourselves caught between inconsistent beliefs, values and ideas? Obviously this dissonance would foster serious consequences in the life of a mixed blood child. From that dissonance we come up with new ideas, beliefs and values that will help minimize the mental conflict we find ourselves in. But in some of those new ideas, beliefs and values can be found self-destruction.

In terms of identity, the mixed blood child who experiences intense rejection from one of their ancestral bloodlines will naturally take into their identity the group that shows acceptance. Thus many mixed bloods will identify as Native while others will identify as white. It is interesting how scholars of Metis people show the early rise of the Metis identities. They explain cultural affiliation as a result of whether or not the European male took his family responsibility seriously. If he remained with the family he brought them into European culture; if he abandoned the family they were forced to return to the mother's band, where her children would grow within the certainty of their Native bond. This is all very well and true, but what happened to the relatives of the children who became Indian or the relatives of the children who became white? I can tell you. Many later rejected their nieces, nephews, uncles, aunties and cousins as being not Indian or not white like them. And the children, what did they do? Rather than blossoming in the beauty of their uniqueness they denied themselves and chose to be one or the other. The rejection of one side or the other is to my way of thinking a perceptual protection, a way to restore cognitive equilibrium – a way to try to become someone – of value.

And so I grew up with siblings whose choices were not mine, but the sad part is our individual choices have caused more division, misunderstanding and fighting.

NO RESPECT
The other day I said "White man"
And you freaked out on me
called me racist said no
wonder no one loved me

Cries From A Metis Heart

who would want someone like you
"Look at the way you talk"
you said to me . . .
"No respect . . . my dad was white
I loved him"
you screamed tears pouring
down your face
No respect!
Well . . . I thought to myself
he was my dad too.
I loved him too
But I didn't want to fight so I
kept silent
today you said "Indian" in
a voice filled with loathing
and contempt
No respect my insides screamed
Our mother was a half-breed
I loved her too
No respect!
I couldn't freak out . . .
So I kept silent . . . but
I know your hypocrisy.
My skin crawls for what you
deny her . . . deny us . . .
the dignity to exist as part "Indian"

Will my sister and I ever come to meeting of souls? I think we will once we come together fearlessly facing what has divided us in the first place, our conditioning by society's stereotypes.

Whenever I dwell on mixed blood's confusion I can't help but be overwhelmed with our multiple losses – losses I often equate with the Wéhtiko, a voracious creature better known as "cannibal," whose lust for consumption is never abated. I call the colonizer a Wéhtiko. He came, he saw, he devoured everything from our land to our bodies to our identities. His history, his religion, his education system, stole our memories and chilled our hearts. We are no longer people of warmth. Oh no, not us. We struggle amid constant hypocrisy and have in many cases become cold, insensitive and isolated from people and most importantly, from our land. We have now become consumers of land as if it were nothing more than a commodity waiting passively for our greed to bleed its very lifeblood.

WHEN
A mother cries
don't rape my child

As flesh is torn
too scarred to heal

My mother earth
I hear your cries

As that Wéhtiko
disguised as white man

forced the water
from your womb

You felt each savage
penetrating thrust

till dry and barren
just a shell

Then I watched
a mother's rage

From tsunamis
To earthquakes

You Wéhtiko . . .
now cringe in fear

Hiding in your tiny hole
feeding off your greed

Where were you when
she fed you

Where were you
where she clothed you

You saw progress
I saw death

You saw money
I saw rape

Now you see death
I see revenge

When a mother cries
don't rape my child

This Wéhtiko also ate our understanding of land's spiritual connection to identity. Today we talk about blood quantum and authentic Indians, authentic Metis, as if blood were the only thing that makes us who we are. Hell, we love to parade the euphemisms of Status, non-status, C-31 and Metis. What about land and its connection to our identities? That European Wéhtiko started separating my ancestors from their ability to create their identities in relationship with the land. It forced abstract names devoid of land's spirit onto connected people. How can Mary, Joe or even Lorraine have any relationship to the land when those names have no connection?

And so began the insidious separation, then God, the man, took over from spirit. God of course lives somewhere other than this land, I believe they call it Heaven, some transcendental place. We give respect to God now instead of the land. We thank God now for what we eat, for *his* bounty, instead of thanking the animals and plants for *their* bounty, that which actually sustains us. We even have personal relationships with this absentee God and we forget the relationship we once had with the spirits that continue to live and breathe in all life. But, our grandmothers knew, our grandfathers knew about:

NORTHERN LIGHTS
The sky sings the music
when our ancestors
come and dance for us.
Greens, pinks, reds, blue
and purple dance to the rhythm
keeping spirits up
when life weighs heavy
The shimmering waves
of wondrous movement

clinging to our grandmothers
and grandfathers singing
softly in our minds
we just have to listen
and they will speak
we just have to watch
and they will come.

Our grandparents are waiting, they are simply waiting for us to come home to remember who and what created our identities before the Europeans forced a new artificial identity upon our ancestors. They want us to remember and begin once again to recreate our identity in relationship with the land. In much the same way, reliving my past experiences, re-examining my perceptions and putting the pain down in print has helped me distance myself from my own debilitating patterns of self-destruction. It gave me an insight into my own wéhtikowatisiwin – that is, my own personal cannibal sickness where I let materialism consume my humanness.

I read in *Misty Lake* (a story about residential schools) that humans need to learn how to suffer, and in order to understand that suffering we have to understand our history; we have to come to know we were not responsible for what happened to us. [15] My process of writing has taught me precisely that; it opened up a world of historical connection. I came to see the interconnectedness of my pain and my life's choices. I saw my children's lives intimately tied to my pain and I saw their choices destroying them much as mine had almost destroyed me. I came to see we had been victims of a past we had not created. As such, I came to see that living with a sense of victimization was not a place I wanted to live. I could visit it, yes, but only long enough to give me guidance, after that I would leave it behind and celebrate my life.

NOTES

9 Historically, in the United States anyone born of an African/white mix was automatically and legally considered black, regardless of how light-skinned they might be, thereby dismissing their white ancestry. No matter how an individual wanted to identify, they were forced into the category of black. In Canada on the other hand, government spent years trying to dissolve Indian status. On drop of Indian blood would never have been enough to be legally recognized as Indian, thereby dismissing the person's legal right to identify as "Indian."

10 Zack Naomi. *Thinking about Race.* Belmont CA: Wadsworth Publishing company, 1998: 5. Zack, *American Mixed Race The Culture of Microdiversity.* Lanham, Maryland: Rowman & Littlefield, 1995, p. *xvii.*

11 Alturo Aldama. "Visions in the Four Directions Five Hundred Years of Resistance and Beyond" in *As We Are Now,* 1997:147.

12 Alfred Arteago. "An Other Tongue." In A. Arteago (ed.) *An Other Tongue: Nation and Ethnicity in the Borderlands.* Durham & London: Duke University Press, 1994: 9-33. See Maria Lugones, "On Complex Communications," in Hypatia 21:3 (2006): 75-85.

13 Autocolonialism occurs when we not only believe the colonizers created representations of ourselves but also we impose them on ourselves. In other words, "(t)he colonizer's language and discourse are elevated to the status of arbiter of truth and reality; the world comes to be as the authoritative discourse says. Our world is define(d) for the benefit of the colonizer." (Arteago, ibid, p. 16)

14 See: Naomi Zack. *Thinking About Race.* Belmont, California: Wadsworth, 1998; Rainier Spencer. "Raced and Mixed Race A Personal Tour" in *As We Are Now: Mixedblood Essays on Race and Identity.* Berkeley, California; University of California Press, 1997.

15 Darrell Racine & Dale Lakevold. *Misty Lake.* Lake Audy, Manitoba: Alder & Ringe, 2000, p.50.

Intergenerational Trauma

2

How does one face the tumult that has descended upon one's own family? I watched as my children suffered a legacy I had inadvertently taught them. It was not my intention to hurt my children. I had grandiose plans of being the best mom in the world, of providing them with all the security and self-esteem they deserved. At least those were my plans. Instead I led them down a path of destruction clothed with love – my inadequate understanding of what love was supposed to be. At times I would buy them everything I could to make up for the little we had. Other times I would deprive them of necessities, justifying my behaviour by fear of not having enough. Sometimes I spoiled them uncontrollably and other times I denied them their rights, usually in inappropriate situations. Discipline was never consistent and depended on my own emotional space and sense of safety. As they grew into the sickness of confusion and rebelled I would withdraw my affections as my mother had, only I called it "tough love" and all the while deluding myself that I was doing what was best for them.

For my children, whether I called it "tough love" or "spoiling them" made no difference, for they could not grasp what love was supposed to be, and like me they learned to walk on eggshells, internalizing when to exploit and when to retreat. The following poems are an expression of my forgiveness to myself for what I brought to them. They are also a testament to the struggles, fears and self-doubts that my children had to endure. For each child there are different stories. The healing of intergenerational trauma is best expressed in recognizing and learning to both forgive and honour myself and my children for the dependency-survival [16] strategies that we adopted.

Thus, it is crucial that I address the issue of child abuse. Clearly my life as a child was filled with child abuse. This is an abuse we all know gets handed down generation to generation; therefore I am guilty of perpetrating my own forms of abuse on my children. This is a pattern I want to end so my grandchildren do not suffer. It is vital that I own what I did regardless of historical legacies. My legacy will help me understand what has happened, but it does not give me permission to avoid my own complicity.

I see abuse all around me and the injustice infuriates me. Yet, I realize we are bringing to our children exactly what was brought to us. How we perceive our duties as parents and how we act on those perceptions is where the abuses continue. My own complicity with abuse cannot be absolved by blaming my history. But, without knowing and acknowledging that history the abuse will not stop. Where to begin the story when it is your children you helped destroy? Let me start with my daughter, my youngest child. I remember when my daughter was sexually abused. I wasn't there for her when she desperately needed me the most. I was blind to what was happening to her. By the time I found out she had already suffered for seven years. I hated and I wanted to kill him, but most of all I hated myself for he was a stranger, a man I brought home and forced into the role of parent to my children. It was a role he was not cut out for. Instead he abused my children, physically with my two boys and sexually with my daughter. For myself there was his ever-present terror of violence. I still cringe when I see his image. I still see the house being smashed up. I can still feel the rush of air as the typewriter flew past my head. I was deathly afraid of him but equally afraid to leave. He always said there was nowhere I could run. I believed him and my children suffered. My children and I subsequently made choices based on the terrifying reality of violence and abandonment.

In the absence of safety my daughter grew in a home of distrust. When her biological father and I divorced he abandoned her along with her brothers. As an adult my baby girl thus found solace wherever she could find it. She searched for love and acceptance and it always eluded her.

My daughter like myself and so many others would bow her head in shame reliving the embrace of a man she never wanted but needed to help her escape for a brief time the memory of her past. I could hear her agony, I could feel her pain, but I could not save her from herself any more than I could have saved myself. She was a young woman whose childhood had been stripped when she was barely five. Women like her who seek comfort in the arms of many men need to know they are not sluts or whores; they were children who were violated by sick perverted men.

I tried to help my daughter see that we can't absolve the lust that raped our faith in men. For some of us we retreat into frigidity, for others, promiscuity, but in both cases we are simply trying to ease the pain of living hell. We find ourselves running away from relationships and into one-night stands, yet there is nowhere we can run without catching up to ourselves, and each time the reflection in our mirror gets uglier and uglier.

Cries From A Metis Heart

My daughter is no different than any other woman who has been robbed of her right to be safe. The betrayal against her ultimately fostered self-destructive patterns of behaviour. Today she has risen above the intensity of her pain. Together we shared our life stories, our deepest secrets and in the process we came to know each other as women. The act of revealing the secrets we carried freed us from a legacy of shame. It showed us a way out of the quagmire of self-hate and blame we had sunk so deeply into. It gave my daughter a chance to live a healthier life, a happier life and a life filled with love. As is common with most trauma, the memory and pain continue to haunt her. This time, however, we share a healthy strategy: we talk it out.

My eldest son found solace in a gang and for years it looked like we had lost him. He turned away from us and built a new family – a family that he truly believed cared about him. He felt a safety with them that he had never felt with us. He knew street life and understood the idea of "watching your back," something his mother had not been able to do with success. He believed his street friends would never abandon him and make him feel alone. The problem is the people watching his back were also hurting others. For my son, the pain of his life could not be buried. He raged at the world. He raged at innocent people and he raged at me.

NOW WHO'S DEAD
I bowed my head in defeat
the day I heard

"You fucken bitch
I hate you."

"I don't have a mother
you are dead"

"Do you hear me
You are dead."

The hatred in your voice
my son will never dim.

One day I sat listlessly
watching television

When the reporter's words
Jolted me wide awake.

National news
assault with a deadly weapon

I heard your name
in disbelief

My son – a man
my baby boy

Boiling rage
is killing him

I wonder now
now who is dead?

My son.

It is easy to condemn our children when they make choices society deems pathological, but these same children were innocent and trusting once till their little hearts were shattered by cruelty.

I heard the rage
erupting and ran in fear
to find
my little boy
his trembling body
hiding underneath the bed
afraid
In horror I watched
the bed lifted and
his tiny frame
dragged out
crying
My screams ignored
he hurt you.
My son
he hurt you
as I stood by
and didn't call for help

Fear of abandonment torments my sons just as it does my daughter. My son wants to show his own sons he will never abandon them and he sees discipline as a form of abandonment, the withdrawal of love, therefore he will not tolerate any discipline of his young sons – that is, until he reaches an internal explosion. Like me, he is inconsistent with discipline, and like me he is passing on a legacy of confusion.

My youngest son had his own demons and he fought on a different level. Being the middle child he felt rejection. He was a quiet child who caused no trouble, therefore he was often forgotten; neglect is the better word. He was always overshadowed by his brother, who by virtue of being first born was special, and a sister who was the only girl. One can only imagine the loneliness and feelings of invisibility this caused him.

He tried hard to become a good father, a loving husband. He gave his all and it looked like he was succeeding. Nonetheless, my youngest son found solace in material satisfaction while isolating himself from his brother and sister. My son learned to withdraw his love, a lesson well learned from the women in his life.

YOUR BROTHER
He rocked your cradle
And sang you songs
"Mama, please don't cry because
your little boy must leave you"
and how you would laugh
comforted in your brother's love.
He panicked when you cried
and ran to get a bottle
thinking milk
would cease your pain
He fed you then.

You watched him and
tried to copy the
older brother you adored
who swaggered showing
off his life
comforted in his brother's love.
Do you remember?
Now you watch with different eyes

and wonder how your big brother
could just walk away from
a little brother who needed him

No one knows the
secrets that your big
brother's life now holds or why
he dreams in pain
and shies away from love
Guessing games of why, why, why
yield little comfort
when you hear he's jailed again
in anger you turn away from a
brother you no longer know

But there was a time
he rocked your cradle and sang
"Mama, oh please don't cry because
your boy must leave you"
Remember when he loved you
remember when he fed you?
Would you also walk away
when he's in desperate need
or can you feed him now
like he once fed you?

My children have suffered equally, but clearly their survival strategies were
somewhat different. For all of us, however, our choices were made in escape mode.
We have suffered, and for all of us we have come full circle to recognition of what
we had stolen from us.

DOLL THEM UP
Doll them up\pretty them up
It's not for you that I bought those clothes
it's for the neighbours
so they'll see what a good mom I am
It's not for you, what do you matter
you can't hurt me, you're only my children
But the neighbours they will see
and that's what really matters

it doesn't matter if our home
is just a house as long as no one
else knows what goes on inside
You . . . you don't matter . . . you are
just my children but others
will talk if I don't dress you right
but you I can keep silent
you don't matter don't you see
you cannot hurt me like others can
so I'll keep my house clean
not because your health matters
but to keep them from hurting me
I'm sorry if you're feeling hurt
abandoned or betrayed
But since you are my children
I trust you all to keep your pain inside
Don't ever let them see you hurt
My children hide yourself
in their image, don't ever look beyond
to find what you think you need

My children learned well from me. They learned how to run. I did not have the skills needed to be a good mom. I tried, but in my attempts lived also my deepest fears and insecurities that I also passed on. My mother taught me a philosophy of silence; I taught my children a philosophy of distrust.

Another generation-to-generation legacy we pass on has to do with sexuality. My daughter learned a lot about her sexual self from a mother who did not understand her own sexuality. My sons learned their sexuality in the absence or domination they witnessed and their significant females' reactions. We were like lost children searching books to give us an idea of who we should be and how we should act and the meaning of love since its very presence was an absence in our home.

SENSUALITY?
I tried to comprehend
sensuality to separate
from merely sex

beyond the world of lust
beyond the world of rape
But what I found
in twisted thought
meant learning to dress right
meant watching how
magazine models could
strut their stuff.
It meant wearing lace and
filmy gossamer fabric
preferably black or red
flowing negligees
It meant wearing a mask

And so I did my best to discover who I was as a woman and found the answer in my older sisters. My daughter, on the other hand, had no older sisters to watch or guide her. Her role models were found in schools where families had money and some semblance of normalcy. My daughter wanted to be like them, but her life offered her nothing like the lives she was watching, and so she ached for what she did not have. She tried her best to fit in to a world beyond our means. She tried to look and be like the girls she was watching at school and faced her own rejection.

I bequeathed my veil of ignorance to my daughter and she internalized the "image."

LONG HAIR
Remember when
You were five?
You loved that little boy
Your first heartbreak
How you cried as
I stroked your flowing hair
I can still hear you

"But mommy, Tommy loves
Beth"
It's OK baby, I said
Still stroking your hair
"but she has short hair"

you cried out
in bewilderment
I remember smiling sadly
at your innocence
Did I teach you
long hair was
beautiful
and not just you?
I always thought
long hair was
seductive
alluring
Today
your words have
come back to tease my
brain as I watch him
in the heat of desire
I see her short hair
And I remember your
innocent pain
confusion thinking
your hair could find
you love
and I know it won't

Where do we find love? Well, it sure isn't in the storybooks I hoarded as a child. All those happily-ever-after endings eluded me, yet I thought they could come true. I held fast to the belief in "happily ever after." I forgot I was not from the world that created the fairy tale.

What did I bequeath my sons? My oldest son hit the streets at a young age. He felt abandoned by his mother. Because of my belief that if I only did better my husband would change, I continued to stay in abusive relationships. As a result, my son believed I did not love him. He saw my loyalty going to husbands rather my children. He felt betrayed by his own mother. He grew up terrified of not being loved. His patterns of behaviour, however, were to attack rather than accept the love that was offered to him. Ironically he has done the very thing he feared the most: he abandoned his own first-born child. He cannot face the truth of his fears. He would not let the world know he had weaknesses. He presented an image of toughness as if that would protect him. He is the one child who would give his shirt off his back to someone else in need but quickly rejects anyone who says "no" to him. Physically he is a grown man, but emotionally he is like a little child throwing tantrums. He is still searching for someone to accept him, but he will not accept himself. Like his mother, he could not trust. The child had no one he could trust and as an adult he acted out his distrust.

My youngest son also learned not to trust. However, instead of raging at the world he turned silent. He learned to rely on no one and internalized rejection. He wears his mask perfectly.

TRAPPED BETWEEN

A mother trapped between
the animosity of her sons
cries in the night
searching for solutions

One so full of life
carries stardust in his eye
He believes in magic
love and faith

The other lost in life
carries bitterness in his soul
He no longer believes in magic
and fears love and faith

One has time for football
and cheers his children on
The other hides behind the shades
and feeds his anger on
the loss of freedom his choices
wrought
One gets high on life
The other just gets high

They no longer speak
mistrust rears its ugly head
driving deeper the wedge
that cuts between them
while cruel words fly without remorse

Flesh of a mother's flesh
Seeks desperately to
reunite what
life has stolen
from her boys
A mother trapped between
the animosity of her sons
prays in the night
and loves them both

What did I bequeath my youngest son? As I already stated, he felt a lot of rejection. People were always moving in and out of our home, so he never came to a place of security. Furthermore, I had a number of marriages, and each time when the abuse became too much I would leave. My quiet son lived in a constant state of insecurity with nowhere to turn and no one to turn to. I believe that my son learned that he had to stay in his relationship no matter the cost to him or his family, for in that way he could prevent his children from experiencing what he experienced as a child. He will not allow his children to feel rejection. He would not abandon them, nor would he allow their mother to abandon them in spite of the fact that she had become dependent on drugs. He held fast to the adage, "till death do we part." While some could call this admirable behaviour, it kept him in denial. He would not confront injustice or the reality of addiction. He does not drink alcohol and does not use drugs; therefore he could not see that he too was hurting his children in other ways. Children need to be protected, and if that means confronting the addict then so be it. Like so many of us, however, he ran from confrontation.

JUNKIE LADY
She is a junkie
a child no longer
needing your
protection
She needs salvation but not from you.
You are too
Dependent
too blind
to see.
Does dependency
mean anything
to you

as children watch
addiction
race across
her arms?

I ache for what I see my children suffer. I know where the suffering comes from. I understand completely what generation-to-generation trauma means. I have watched it weave through my family. I listened as my mother told her own stories, so I know she passed on to me what I passed on to my children. I have watched it nearly destroy us. I am still watching as it wraps its tentacles around my grandchildren. But this is where it stops. It will stop because we will not stay silent anymore.

NOTES

16 Most people consider dependency a negative trait. However, if we really think about it, while they are in fact negative, many of our dependencies have actually allowed us to survive. Therefore we should be able to forgive ourselves for becoming dependent on others, or for abusing ourselves with drugs or alcohol.

Don't Rape My Child
3

Where does one begin to talk about sexual abuse? The very notion of sexual abuse is abhorrent in and of itself, but when it comes in the form of family violation it becomes a bogeyman, a monster we know about but chose not to believe in. Too many times the victim remains silent, afraid of being ostracized, afraid of being hurt by speaking out.

> Can I hear my own voice
> am I also invisible to myself?
> Who will hear me if I can't?
> Why can't I want me?
> Who am I, who was the
> little girl alone crying
> Who was the little girl
> scared to be alone at night
> afraid of prying hands
> searching for something
> she knew not what?
> Who was that little girl?

The perpetrator remains powerful and sick and never has to pay for his crimes. Crimes against a child cause a lifetime of shame. The child who remains silent takes that shame into her/his being and it infects every part of their life. Incest – let's call it what it is – eats at us from the inside to the out. My son when he heard about his sister said it was more than a violation of her body; it was having his sister's life stolen from her. He was right! I know because my life was also stolen from me and it took more than 40 years to face this fact. My daughter and I learned to suffer shame and guilt and as a result, love, and trust that elusive something or other was also denied to us, denied by our own trapped minds, trapped in the belief that we were worthless, unlovable and undesirable. I know from talking to them that my sons carried a similar sense of worthlessness, thus my sons learned a deep rage and helplessness that trapped in their minds.

I truly believe my children and I suffered from sexual terrorism. Sexual terrorism lives in the total destruction of a woman's understanding of sexuality, sensuality and sex, of her very being. It is the total destruction of her ability to negotiate safe and healthy relationships, where being beaten is fairly normal. It is about the terror of living with one's self. It means living with self-hatred, self-disrespect and constant condemnation for her living history. It means living with every mistake and letting the mistakes grow cancerous on the soul. It means letting the cancer envelop every aspect of the woman's life. It means letting the cancer spread to her children and their children.

I've always thought *cancerous* was an apt term for those suffering sexual terrorism. It is an unseen disease yet it festers and spreads while slowly killing the inside body. It can incapacitate us emotionally, mentally and physically. We may or may not be able to have normal bodily responses to desire. We may reject ourselves as healthy sexual beings or we may try to absolve the sin against us by overindulging in sexual activities as if to convince ourselves that we were to blame for what happened to us. Sometimes, as we grow older we learn to fight back. Sometimes we never learn; we just run into relationship after relationship, never understanding why and always blaming ourselves for another failure.

Even when we learn to fight back at a minimal level we nonetheless experience a lifetime of nightmares. Thus, the strength that should have been ours is reduced to desperation and we do not see that we are strong, courageous and survivors!

I knew the terror of hands sneaking beneath the blanket to touch a little girl. I knew the terror that taught the child to pretend to be asleep. I knew the terror of not objecting, keeping silent, deathly afraid of what came next. I knew my body was up for grabs for whoever wished to claim it. I knew the faces . . . cousins, uncles who invaded my secret places.

By the age of six I already knew there was no such thing as safety. By the age of 17 I was well versed in my lack of value. But I fought back one day. I don't know how or why. One day that man they called my uncle pulled my jeans open and tried to slip his hands inside. My body shook with a frightening intensity and my heart pounded mercilessly as I cried in desperation, no, no, please no. I struggled fiercely against his groping hands. With bile rising I clung ferociously to keep my jeans in place. No more . . . no more, I screamed. I fought back that day. I know the terror now that tells me what to do.

So we can learn to fight back, but where does the fighting take us? Too often it denies an ability to have healthy relationships. Always in the deepest

Cries From A Metis Heart

recesses of the mind lives the ghost of what happened and what could happen again. Too often we freeze and deny ourselves the right to feel physical and emotional pleasure.

Why does your body frighten me?
Why does your warmth
send me running in distress?
Why do I hide my fear?
Because . . . because . . . because
I remember hands that stole in the night
a young girl's dream

I remember the fingers that
penetrated her soul and froze her flesh
I remember, Oh God, I remember
too many nights denied
forced pleasure of release
Fingers crawling viciously
I remember I hurt
remember his touch
remember the burning filth
that penetrated deep inside

I am ashamed, I tremble
I must not lose control
Damn it body don't ache
don't want to be fulfilled

Don't hide, remember
I want his touch
I want his need
But I remember other nights

Flee to safety
inside your shell
from passion not controlled
Please . . . please . . . please
remember or it will
happen again

Lorraine Mayer

I want his touch
but fingers terrify me
I can't tell him
I don't have the words
I want his need
but memory betrays me
I was just a child . . . now
a woman without love

So this child learned to internalize violation. She carried it throughout her life like a blanket of protection. But her blanket kept out all warmth.

To love a man
to crave his warmth
are places I don't trust

But what would it mean
to be excited by a smile
to long for physical touch?

Is love real
an emotion out of control
a longing for oneness

Where does friendship
end and love begin
in simple conversation?

Electric sensation
faltering words
trust beyond all hope

I suppose it'd make
some women swoon
I don't believe . . .

in myths

What is this new myth? The myth is the idea that love cannot exist for this woman-child. She is unworthy of respect and nurturing. She does not deserve to be held and comforted. Even if she does come to believe she deserves it she will act as if she doesn't and run from any hope that love may find her. Instead she lives with her silence and cries.

SILENCE
Silence
unfolds beneath your green
scent soaking through the flesh
of life
sanctifying
purifying
cleansing far beneath
the echoes of your lust

Silence
deafening pounding in my veins
awakes forgotten time
a savage
thrust of night
Permeates
ameliorates
your ghostly inclinations

Silence
shrouded in the mystery of a gaze
too long entrapped
screaming
betraying
releasing
a flight along the air
despair

I dwelled on possibilities, yet feared them always. I could not seem to escape the torment of a mind and body wanting so much and a spirit afraid to trust. It's like the memories had been grafted to my flesh and I could not forget.

NIGHT STALKER
Darkness enshrouds
with a cold damp cloak
Shivering fear
steals silently through

my body
Alone the night
takes over imagination
Living shadows
grasping – reaching out
to freeze my mind
The night is my stalker
stealthily blocking
my mind
from its own swift flight
to safety
Alone without a friend
In the cold dark night.

NIGHT RANT
Whiskey breath, hot sour lips
slow caresses over troubled flesh
Stop – the silent whisper
echoes dead in night
as children weep their innocence
Raped by vacant eyes
desire, greed, lust, cruelty
draws the child to limbo
found in bed – dead
Vacant eyes, mock the silence
bloodless hands steal her soul
Who to tell – who to tell?
Does no one care
will love find a way
through the maze of shame

My sexual violence has also infected my sons. They are not immune to sexual rejection or violation of their manhood. One son believes he must be macho – the tough guy, never showing weakness. He brags about conquests, but he is a scared little boy. As a child he was physically abused and he will not allow anyone to hurt him again. He mocks his younger brother for showing gentleness. My younger son is normally a gentle man, considerate and caring, but he is terrified of rage. As a child he would cry rather than confront

Cries From A Metis Heart

anything. When he was about six years of age he sat at the dinner table without eating. When questioned about why he wasn't eating he started to cry. In angry frustration I asked why he was crying. Through his tears he stammered, "I don't have a fork." He could not simply ask for a fork. He was terrified of the consequences of asking for something so mundane, something that was his right to have. How did he get this way? He saw what happened when his older brother would question or assert himself. He learned not to assert or ask for anything. He grew up afraid of consequences, thus he will not confront injustice. Like his older brother he presents toughness. His toughness, however, is a different kind of toughness. It comes from presenting a silent, lone individual, not needing anyone. Both my boys are in truth scared little boys, unsure of who they are and what their manhood should be. Both sons have demonstrated an intense dependency on their wives; they need their wives to be there for them like their mother wasn't. In many ways, they have both become their mother.

There have been times when I have raged at the violation to my children and myself, and times when I realized I was punishing myself for what others did. Then finally my rage would be directed outwards.

PALE SLIPPERY ILLUSION
I know you
You are just a pale slippery
illusion of man
You spent yourself
sliding out beneath
the body of my life
leaving me with a
vacant emptiness
feeling only your
pulsating fluid graining
over rotting flesh
Oh yes, I know you
mysterious pale illusion
of man
Who am I to condemn
you ask?
The Indian woman
left forgotten
to bleed alone over

ever-reddening earth
as you stole stealthily out
each night
lost in your foreign greed
Pale slippery illusion
of white man, pretending
to be human
But I remain and
without your shadow
the scars will heal
the emptiness will fill
my flesh breathing life
back to
the body of my soul
Pale slippery illusion
of man,
colonizer,
enemy
friend, lover
I have banished . . . you

It was at times like this when I would write of violation and direct the anger at the source where it belongs that I would find solace; I would begin to trust myself. If only I could stay in a place of safety and trust for myself. But too often I found myself wearing a mask. I would pretend to the world that all was well. But in truth I knew my inner madness. I knew my madness and I could not escape from it.

I want to cry
but force myself
away from tears
Too long in your company
reminders of friendship
lost amid the fears
of yesterday

Tomorrow brings another
day of forcing feelings
past the surface of
your gaze

I live in solitude
hoping you cannot see
what you've forced me to quiet

How many more days
must I endure the pain of
regret, of silence of fear
Of knowing no one cares
where I walk as long as
my walk keeps their path
safe from my feelings

I cannot ignore the pain of betrayal that follows sexual abuse. Nor can I ignore my own betrayal to myself. The choices I have made to escape myself, the other, to find some form of comfort from my agony have often resulted in more self-disgust, more inner contempt and no compassion for the survival strategy that fostered my actions.

BRINGING DOWN THE MOON

She walks her own betrayal
in agony of her lost shattered ego
Easy prey to beckoning arms
Struggling to see his face
pretend against his body
Then stumbles past the ghost
she leaves behind
Another night
a one-night stand
her dignity betrayed

Before the day dawns
the woman that sought
relief from loneliness
will avoid the nightly glow
of grandmother moon
a forgotten memory of
who the woman once was
"Come home, come home"
The silent unheard grandmother's
plea filters through the forest leaves

Lorraine Mayer

"Come home, come home"
She can't run far enough
in terror fleeing through the chill
knowing no way to shed her guilt
of passion once again supplied by
another man . . . a stranger
How can she return home?
lost childhood dreams
cannot come home

By the time the ferns kiss
the mist of morning
and loneliness expels her victory
Another night of emptiness
seductively wrapped in
the arms of gratification
will have claimed another woman
and across her waning cheeks
tears will flow silently

Following my failed marriages I decided to stay out of relationships, since clearly I could not make healthy choices. However, I arrived one day at a point where I wanted love, I wanted it desperately. But still it evaded me. I had worn my cloak of protection for so many years that none could see past it. They saw an angry woman, a cold woman. They did not see a woman in need, a woman desirable, a woman capable of loving others. While these feelings stem from my early abuses, the feelings in and of themselves are felt by many Metis women as we struggle to be seen. Images of beauty have for too long been dominated by Euro-white standards. So if we do not look like miniature Barbie dolls there is something wrong with us.

BARBIE
Barbie was no angel
Bloodsucking thief
Draining dignity from
Lost, little, chubby
Dark hair, pigment wrong
Girls.

The airbrush perfection in magazines carries another illusive image of what a woman should look like. These images are impossible to achieve, especially if you are from a culture that spawns less than white skin. Sexual rejection comes from many places and one particularly hurtful area is that of the men from your own culture. When the men from your culture turn their eyes to beauty they quite often focus on the white woman. So what is left for the Metis or other Aboriginal women? We are left with deep feelings of inadequacy.

I want to scream
at you
Look at me,
see me
I am a woman
I have needs
But you look
past me
to someone else

We watch our men being drawn to women from another world and we hurt. We feel betrayed and too often we internalize their preferences as something wrong with us. We learn to hate our looks. Our imagined inadequacy becomes really real as one after another of our men fall for women not us, and men not of our culture disrespect us.

Your nearness
overwhelms my
senses
Your scent
surrounds me
till I stagger
in unfulfilled
lust
But you do not
see me
You do not feel me
I am invisible
not woman
not desirable
Not anything.

It is strange how our men while rejecting us as sexual women find comfort in our friendship. They are willing to be for there us, to help us in friendship yet deny us what we really need – their love.

You asked nothing
just gave your all
and I believed in you
I loved you
You said someday
It would be my
turn to return
the favour of your
being there for me
And now
you call in the favour
I know I owe
I know I owe
I know
I owe
But I never asked you
to sacrifice your
heart for me.

How do women recover from rejection of the cultural self when our men make clear their preference is for white women? For myself I found solace in writing and a deep internal rage. In writing I could scream and rant without fear of exposing my vulnerability. In terms of my rage I could target someone other than myself for my insecurity.

Night after night
I pound these
keys incessantly
trying to escape
the depth of
my desire for
a man who cannot
see me as
I need to be seen
Who cannot hear me
as I need to be heard
Who cannot hold me
as I need to be held
Who cannot love me

Cries From A Metis Heart

as I need to be loved
So I pound my computer
keys in agony
feeling no relief
from wanting
needing
needing
wanting   .

When the pain of isolation and alienation finally became too much I found
myself in despair and would cry in secrecy.

Cry...
Cry...
Cry...
Cry...
It's OK
it means
you're human

Sometimes I wished I could be anything other than a human. I did not
want to see with more than my eyes. I did not want to feel the intensity of
loneliness. But I cannot go back to a time of blissful ignorance. I see and I
must deal with what I see and know. I also know that years of cultural rejection, sexual rejection and sexual abuse have all culminated in the building of
protective armour and walls. I know I have built many walls to protect myself.
It is not enough to simply blame the men from my culture for their rejection. So
now I question how to tear down the walls that have for so many years kept me
safe. The walls I constructed to keep violators out have also prevented others
from seeing me, and I remain invisible.

The most frightening thoughts I have these days are how to undo what I
have spent years creating, protecting. I understand the depth of my violations. I
understand I did not cause these things to happen to me. I know I was a victim
of sick leches and historical distortions. I know my history, but knowing is not
enough, although it is a necessary beginning. Change is far more difficult, and
I must keep a constant vigil over my thoughts. I must not let my tendency to
second-guess destroy me. Second-guessing every move, word or gesture others
make was a necessary skill to avoid further violation. This skill however, is no
longer a helpmate; it is destructive. It prevents me from taking chances, from

trying to trust, from opening myself up to others. In other words, it is preventing me from experiencing the wonder of life as a sexual person, a nurturing person and woman worthy of loving and being loved. I want to be able to dream.

OCEAN'S TIDE
I gave my dreams
to the ocean one day
to ask if
they ever would
come true
as foolish humans can
But the ocean, it laughed
and mocked my gesture
then rolled my
dreams out to sea.

Death Be Not Silent
4

Death, the balance of life. is something no family can escape. It is something we all understand although we suffer and reject our understanding when it happens. The despair that follows physical death is terribly painful and as much as we grieve we know death is absolute. Emotional death that does not follow from the physical is a form of death we can no longer keep silent. Non-physical death makes no sense; it is the death of the soul or spirit possibly, even the mind. It is a death that walks in a living body. It is the death of belief, of hope. Such death is crushing and our minds refuse to work with it because it should not happen.

In terms of physical loss, I lost a number of relatives when I was still a child. Grief came but it was brief, for it followed with deaths of relatives remote from me. So while I watched my mom and dad suffer I did not appreciate the depth of their grief. In my personal life death reared its ugly head along with terrible guilt when my baby son died in 1978.

THE ABSOLUTE
Sitting on the side
of my bed I
did not move,
I could not move.
A numbness had
overtaken my
body, my brain
Time and sound ceased.
The scream inside
my head unheard
the baby, the baby,
oh God the baby
is dead.

It was then that I experienced non-physical death so intimately connected to the physical that it kept me silent and in terror and guilt for many, many years. I lost my child and the experts said it was from Sudden Infant Death Syndrome. But I thought I knew better. I believed he died from a broken heart. How could he not, when his mother was emotionally absent the four brief months of his existence? For many years I struggled with my guilt, believing he died because of who I was and what I'd done. I could not understand SIDS, but I could certainly understand rejection. Unfortunately for me, his loss came at time in my life when I was being overwhelmed with hypocrisy and deception. I had all but given up and wanted nothing more of life than revenge. But I was pregnant and had an obligation to my unborn child, so for a time I simply waited and planned. I planned my revenge in the arms of another man. My life's choices at that time were destined to rob me of all pride, which escalated when my baby died and I had nowhere to run or anyone to turn to.

SPIRALING SOUL

A torrent of
nightmarish loss
rushes in my veins.
My child is dead
the baby is dead
I'm aching,
fighting to scream
a desperate plea
help me please
help me
But shadows block
my words
from exit –
for sympathetic words
there is no entry
blackness begins
to overtake my mind
With trembling fingers
I clutch
for a breath of sanity
feeling pain slice through
my body
like a jagged dagger

ripping
a path across
the void as a
deafening silence
covers your tiny body.
Within its velvet casket
your flesh will release
your soul to soar
among the stars
while I remain
embracing the
pain by
releasing my spiraling
soul to a
downward crypt
of despair.

People tried to console me, but I couldn't hear them. I could only hear the voice inside hammering incessantly that I was to blame for his death. I wept at what I saw as hypocrisy. I raged at what I saw as insincere. The depth of my grief and the pain of guilt caused me to miss the truth in human compassion. I could not see it and I refused to let it enter my world.

DEATH BE NOT LOUD
Death be not loud
cries silent grief
Don't tell me how I'm strong
while you force-feed me
from a dish of empty sympathy
Don't fucken tell life goes on
I know this fact of life
just let me feel without
demanding
explanation
Wave after wave. hypocrisy
baptizing way to deep
the flesh that crawls with grief.

For more than 20 years I let guilt plague me. Why, because I had been out drinking, trying to get revenge against a husband who had cheated on me over and over. I had begged my mom to let me leave him after his years of infidelity left me a shell of a woman.

My mother was a strict Catholic and she held closely to her beliefs. The very idea of leaving a husband was abhorrent in the eyes of God, the Church and my mom. She refused to see the anguish I carried and insisted that I "had made my bed so now must sleep in it." Distraught, I vowed revenge; I knew no other way out. I wanted to hurt my husband like he had hurt me. I wanted him to know what it was like to be humiliated so publicly. I wanted his manhood to suffer as my womanhood had suffered at his hands. I wanted revenge, but stayed with him. It would have been easier on all of us if I'd had belief in a woman's right to leave.

I was fond of saying that the day my mother screamed at me that "who do you think you are? Do you think you are better than any other woman? I never left your dad," was the day I died a non-physical death. Years later I began to understand what my mother had endured, how much she had denied and how much it must have hurt her, but on that day I simply placed my head in my hands in defeat. I knew I would not leave my husband. Somehow I had to become a better wife; it must have been my fault he cheated so much. I silenced the voice inside that whispered he was in the wrong and convinced myself that I was the problem. Years later I finally did divorce and of course my mother said I was going to go to hell. But, it did not matter anymore since I knew I was already living in hell.

I do not believe I am destined to go to hell regardless of how my life has turned out. Years later, in October 2002, I lost another son, this time from a drug overdose. He was not my biological child but a stepson from my second marriage. I loved him and this time I was able to grieve without feeling personal guilt, but my grief was no less intense. I raged at injustice. I raged at drug use, at drug dealers, at dependency on drugs. I raged and raged and raged at life that steals our families. Drugs had killed him. I felt myself living in a volcano about to explode.

PRESSURE VALVE
Stumbling through the mist
of pain submissive
broken spirit mother
Stand tall one more time
march in time with strain
Another day, another collar

Cries From A Metis Heart

choking down the fear
of facing one more day
Forcing one more smile
upon a world too wrapped
up in *rush* to see your
empty eyes, your cries
While silent screams wrench
uninvited from your dreams
tic toc, tic toc
tic toc . . .
Pressure valve tightening life
waiting patiently to explode
giving birth to death.

While I did not personally feel guilt for his death I nonetheless felt the hopelessness of our future. I also internalized shame. If we were not the people we were I thought this would not have happened to us. For many years it seemed I waited, just existed for more grief. I lost my father from cancer in 1988 and my mother from gangrene in 2003. I felt the despair that follows, knowing the extent to which our health is at risk. Since I am a firm believer in the interconnectedness of mind-body-spirit I fully believed their sicknesses had risen from a cancerous life of hatred, violence, suspicion and bigotry, and none more so than my younger brother.

In 1982 I took my children and ran away from home, but really I was running from my brother. I had experienced many of his violent rages and I did not believe I could ever be safe living near him, so I moved to another province and eventually another country before I felt any measure of safety. I returned to Canada in 2004 and in January 2006 I found he had a massive heart attack.

WAITING BROTHER
The clock ticks once more
The tubes fill your vacant
shell of a body as you
lie there waiting, waiting.
for what for death?
For life to come back to you?
We sit waiting too
Do you know we're here?
Can you feel the breathing

of our fear as your heart
beats an unsteady tattoo
in that machine that clocks
your life.
Can you hear the hushed whispers?
Sisters come from far and near
to gaze upon your face
and then we watch the clock ticking
as the machines keep time
with your energy or
does your energy keep
time with the machines?
We're waiting for you to
know us . . . I think
Maybe you already do?
Your voice has been silenced
by the pattern of your heartbeat
but we wait anyway
You've waited a long time
for us to wait for you
and now you don't even
know we came

There is so much confusion when a sibling hangs on to life by the slimmest
of threads. More so when that sibling has caused so much pain and anguish for
his brothers and sisters. We are caught between fear of losing him and fear of
having him back. Then the betrayal of the mind haunts our thoughts.

GOODBYE MY BROTHER
I can still feel your fist
crushing my face
spewing my blood
wounding my spirit
I can still feel your rage
I want to run
escape
be safe
but I've run too many
years without release

from the feelings of pain
the bitterness that shrouds
my thoughts of you
...
I saw you last lying
cold in that bed
with a heart that refuses
to pump life
and I was scared
But I still felt your fist, I
heard your rage inside my head
I tremble
knowing you're leaving us
and I am afraid
I want to love you
I want to cry for you
But I still feel your rage
...
It was silent in the room
though I still heard your voice
but now it's without
your rage
I tremble
now confused
you go where
none can follow
And now
the phone dangles
There is no more rage
from you for me
from me to you
Goodbye my brother

And then it was over, a month of anxious waiting, watching, hoping and fearing. A month of tiptoeing around siblings, afraid they would guess I really cared when I didn't want to, or that I didn't care when I really wanted to. Then the ominous ring of a telephone letting me know, setting us free, causing us sorrow, confusion denial and taking a brother we should have been able to love.

I cannot cry
the tears of grief
You should not be going
My mind says it over
and over
A sister's love
says you can't leave
it's not time
you are too young
The phone is ringing
if I don't answer
maybe it won't be real
It can't be real
I just talked with you
was it only yesterday?
I'm sure you heard
I saw a tear
My brother I said
don't go, it's too soon
we haven't talked
we haven't forgiven
But you didn't listen
to me
you never did

I helped plan his funeral, the brother I had hated for so long and learned to love too late. I helped with his funeral, numb and confused by my caring. If there is anything I learned through the past years, however, it is that that my brother, like the rest of us, was a victim of a legacy he did not chose. He suffered in rage and as a result faced rejection from the very people who may have loved him back to health. But we could not because we had been conditioned to say nothing, to pretend, to walk away from him.

But to each other we said plenty. Where did it all begin? What spawned the fear so deep that we would walk away from confrontation with our own brother? In fact, walk away or become aggressive and hostile in our confrontations? I searched through my memory to understand, and I found what I believe spawned my terror. Is it possible to remember as far back as being only two years of age? Was it the broken broom or an aunty being dragged from the house? When did the parties end and the violence begin? As I searched my memory I began to wonder if there was ever a time when our family came together in friendship and security. Possibly not.

But trying to make sense of everything is very difficult, especially when trying to write in chronological order. Fortunately, I had the houses we lived in, and they could tell me where I was and when. Then again, I have so many brothers and sisters that remembering their ages resituates me in time and place. Yet, I had to ask myself, did I want to be resituated? Did I want to remember? Did I want to speak about it all? Did I want to strip away the layers of secrecy, pain and guilt? Of course not; no one wants to reopen old wounds or try to find new ones. However, I had no choice; for me, there was no other way to pave the way to security. No one was going to spend millions of dollars restructuring my life or the lives of my children and their children and their children to come.

So what spawned the feeling of terror that lived in my life all those years and plagues me off and on today? I first recalled the violence in 1955 on Logan Avenue. My aunty, I remember seeing her fighting, screaming . . . and then I saw police dragging her along the floor all the while she was kicking and screaming. I don't know what she did, but I saw what the police did. This tiny child watched and heard the deafening noise, the tones of rage and despair. The child was so terrified and there was no one there to help her because they were fighting, with arms and fists everywhere. The presence of children is forgotten when grownups become crazy. The child wanted the noise to stop, she wanted someone to hold her, reassure her, but the grownups were drawing blood and no one could help her understand what was going on. She learned to put her own context to the sights, the noise and the fear. And at an early age she learned to walk with stealth around a certain rage and humbly beg forgiveness when the deafening noise began. The child learned to hide despair behind a smiling face. The child then taught her children to hide behind a silent hurt in trembling fear, and forgot what happens to children when grownups become crazy. And so her children learned too to place the pain behind the mask.

Children internalize what they don't understand. As I said, one of my brothers became a violent man. As for myself, I was able to take noise, loud noise, and it became my constant teacher. I would run if anyone expressed even the remotest anger. I would do anything to stop someone from getting angry with me. The visual memory of my aunt and the police stayed with me. I don't know which was worse; being afraid people would not love me if they were angry or afraid of being hurt by their anger. My mother would withdraw her love when she was angry – emotional blackmail, some would call it. She used to tell me she had stopped taking her diabetes medicine because she was angry at something one of us had done. In that way, she said, "I'll show you kids." I internalized anger as incompatible with love. But, I also learned to use emotional blackmail.

I did not know anger could be justified. I did not know it was OK to get mad. I thought these were emotions that were part of a sick, deranged person. I did not want to be sick and I did not want anyone thinking me deranged. so I buried any evidence of anger toward all but children. I believed anger would get me hurt. Obviously I was learning to shut down feelings that for other people are normal expressions of life. The fact that I could express anger toward children frightened me and I would sometimes retreat into emotional blackmail to avoid expressing anger. I saw all anger as the prelude to abuse. But emotional blackmail, what was wrong with that? No one was getting beaten or screamed at so it must be OK. For me, the normal became a threat and I buried feelings like I later buried my grief.

I still find it difficult at times to accept anger or rage as anything other than abnormal. My intellectual brain understands full well the implications of feelings and the need to express oneself. But, my emotional self, maybe my unconscious self, continues to fight against getting angry. How do I manage such a strategy? Well, when someone wrongs me I look to myself for the source of the blame. Thus, rather than seeing another violation of sorts I see myself as wrong, bad, useless and so on. In other words, I internalize the anger and direct it at myself. In this I am safe, for I cannot abandon myself. This type of behaviour is nothing more than the death of the self. This I learned from a long legacy of violence, of denial, of silence and of protection.

MY SISTER DO YOU REMEMBER
My sister do you remember
the small cramped kitchen?
The woodstove made good pies
and, the rose-coloured room
most people call dining room
We bathed in tubs there
oldest to youngest
Scrubbed clean with the other's dirt.
Remember the blue room?
ha, the living room
robin's-egg blue mom

used to say with pride, she
loved them birds didn't she?
Do you remember the neighbours?
the Germans and Italians next door
or the egg man down the street
the corner store up the road
oh that road I remember
how the stones kept dust from
clogging the cars.
a good idea till little brother
visited the rocks with his tongue
A quick visit to the hospital
good thing uncle was home.
Remember walking down the back alley
how mom hated to be seen
lugging her meagre groceries
with each child carrying its share.
Do you remember the Virgin
hanging beside the phone
mom loved that picture
there was robin's-egg blue
in that one too.
I can still smell the bannock
we had to hide when people
came to visit and the raisin pie
we could let them see.
I remember so much, about as
much as I guess I forgot.
The rose bushes smelled good
The caraganas where we buried our pets
and the old maple tree I wanted
to live in crying like a baby
when that Italian man cut the branches.
Do you remember the attic?
You lived there once I know
The cellar all dank and terrifying
little brother's prison . . .
can't believe they would

imprison a child.
I remember his fear I smelled it
I heard it . . . I cried
I remember so much I want
to forget
I hate robin's-egg blue

There are so many ways in which we can die a non-physical death. Watching the horrendous abuse perpetrated on ourselves, our brothers and sisters. Feeling the absolute helplessness to stop the pain and abuse. I have living memories of seeing my younger brother locked in a cellar as punishment. I remember the attic where my older sister was banished so no one would find out she was pregnant. I remember so well, the horror of those prisons. Today that would be called severe child abuse, but for us it was part of our parent's discipline. Death of trust can only follow such forms of discipline. Without trust how does a child learn to survive? As I have said before, we survive by adopting strategies that are self-destructive. We punish ourselves for what others have wrought.

Another form of death comes from denial of history, of ancestry, of memory. In order to protect ourselves from discrimination and further abuses we may distance ourselves from our families or our ancestry. We can bury memory so it will not plague us in our waking moments. The problem with this type of burial is that it comes back to haunt us in our sleep.

I LEFT THE HOUSE
I heard the wind again
last night
calling me back to
years ago.
I saw you stroll
among the pines
carefree and alive.
I heard you
I smelled you
I knew you
my ancestor.
I felt the rain this
morning
wash away the
memory.

Cries From A Metis Heart

Five hundred years
of history
forgotten
in the concrete world
I walk today.
And then I left
the house.
No one hears you
no one smells you
you are invisible
as I struggle to exist
in the world without you
Mother
Grandmother
Great-grandmother.

Colonization, racism and discrimination have played a significant role in denying, distorting and separating us from pride in ourselves as Aboriginal people. It has left a terrible death, emotionally and spiritually. However, it is not impossible to be reborn. I am not talking about rebirth from a Christian conversion. I am talking about rebirth of our ancestry. We can learn to take back our ancestry. We can come to see it in its fullness and beauty. We can learn to see it with pride and to wear it with honour. We can overcome the deepest trauma and despair of guilt resulting from physical death. We can also be reborn from death that is non-physical. We can and we are!

Binding the Sash
5

I've spent many years coming to terms with Metis history, our losses, our trials and our rejection by others. For me, "Biding the Sash" is about recovery, and taking back pride. In the old days our ancestors used the L'assumption sash in many practical ways, from keeping body heat evenly distributed to pulling Red River carts out of boggy areas. I have been told it was only the men who wore the sash. Today women are also wearing the sash; they do so to demonstrate unity and pride. For many of us, showing unity and pride is a relatively recent phenomenon, mainly because years of discrimination by anyone not Metis inhibited such displays. Nonetheless, we are still the people who bind the sash, metaphorically symbolizing the holding together of a nation, a nation that no one can take away from us. The sash can also help us bind families together and to bind new friendships cross-culturally.

TO THE JESUIT'S GRANDSON
Your ancestors brought us Christianity
400 years ago you would
have been here to convert me
so,
how come we are friends
was it an accident of history
that made you my friend and
not my missionary
so,
could it be your ancestors
had been my ancestor's friend
where were you 400 years ago
I know I was here
Was I waiting for you
to finally become a friend
I remember well the crass
cold metal dangling from your hip

Beads rolling through your fingers
In contempt you beheld the savage man
but lust in your eyes raped his child
so,
was your ancestor my ancestor's friend
History weaves a subtle pain in your heart
not guilty you cry – I wasn't there
I am your friend you say
so,
are you claiming
your eyes won't rape my child
Your greed won't steal her home
Contempt you say has changed to
Warmth – to love – to friends
Maybe – maybe
Yes, maybe – you are my friend

The constant battle Metis people have to undergo still amazes me. In 2006, for example, the Manitoba Metis Federation went to court fighting a land claim – a land claim that should have been resolved in favour of the Metis when Manitoba first became part of Canada.[17] We have spent our entire history fighting for acknowledgment: from Cuthbert Grant's battle to maintain Metis rights in the pemmican trade, to Louis Riel's bid for the right to self-governance to Gabriel Dumont's last stand at Batoche. Yet, in spite of years of outstanding feats and defeats we still have scholars like Flanagan who believe we do not have the right to exist as Aboriginal people.[18]

FLANAGAN
A white lady once said
to me
"you should be happy
Europeans came and
mixed their blood with yours
otherwise
you would still be ugly."

Bitch!
Now Flanagan, he says
Canada made a mistake
there is no such thing

Cries From A Metis Heart

as Metis rights 'cause
they have European blood
These white folks like to
talk about blood, at least
when it is theirs.

Ol' Flanagan he says,
we bought their Euro ways.
How many times must
we be denied?
we carry other blood
Why can't it be my Indian blood
that provides my element
of beauty?

What of our First Nations
blood?
I believe it counts for
something.
It wasn't European blood
that gave us soft brown skin.
It wasn't just European
language that blended made
Michif

It wasn't Euro skills that taught us
how to hunt, to trap
to know animals
to survive within the bush
It wasn't European ways
that taught us to love our mothers
and not see them as chattel.
It wasn't Europeans
who granted Mother Earth
the right to live
for her own sake

But now the European
descendent chooses

to dismiss us as legitimate
people,
a Nation
just because we carry Euro blood
but remember ... it is NOT
in isolation in our bodies or
in our lives

Then people wonder why we get so damned angry.

It doesn't really matter
does it?

If it is a wobbly shanty on
the side of the road

Or worn-out lumber cabin sitting
in the middle of the bush

Fancy clothes or patches
welfare line or politicians' hill

Can't silence voices of contempt
for my people

How much more rage can I endure
without my body exploding

In your face
then you ... "Oh dear Canada" can

Condemn another Metis

I guess scholars like Thomas Flanagan can dismiss Canada's treachery, but we cannot. Our families carry the memory on tiny pieces of paper. We carry Canada in our ancestry. We carry the lies, the deceit.

SCRIP[19]
A tiny piece of paper
forged by government
to seduce the land
from me

hesitate, prevaricate
the process
till homeless Metis
left confused

those marketers
so newly come
swooped in like pirates
lusting after gold

for love of wealth
these swindlers
offered rotten bait
to steal our land

from helpless children
their legacy,
their identity
denied

by government officials
bureaucrats and law
and now we sing O Canada
our home and native land

but I remember scrip
I remember
Manitoba
and I remember 1870

There is so much beauty and perseverance in being Metis. There is however also ugliness – an ugliness we inherited from cultural denial and abuse. It is no secret that we Metis people found ourselves justifying our existence by retreating into either an Indian or a white identity. Then when we finally come together as a people we still find reason to withdraw or fight among ourselves. We are no less prone to political battles than any other cultural group, yet when we fight among ourselves it gets sensationalized.[20] The release of the infamous *Rotten to the Core*[21] certainly attests to how appealing it is to discredit any Metis.

METIS MADNESS
Someone must have mentioned money

'cause greed does funny things
It summons ancestry out of graves
when years were left forgotten
ignored or consciously abandoned
for the privilege of being white
But someone must have mentioned money
'cause the ground is shaking underneath
the feet rushing in to claim their past.

Did fiddles sing you to sleep at night?
Were hides wrapped round your tiny body
to keep you safe and warm?
Did Michif confuse
your English-speaking mind?
I have no argument with ancestry
forcibly denied till found
or recovery of spirit.
But to say you are
what you have never been
'cause you denied
your own brown skin
is going way too far.

What is this Metis madness
that beckons fledgling heirs
And, what is this Metis madness
that denies their right to be?
What is this Metis madness
that makes us seek to
right the wrong that tears
apart sisters, brothers, kin?
This Metis madness
is having
leaders who believe and those
with simple faith
in their might
to protect
their legacy of land.

There is strength in belonging. We once had that strength. Today however, we are confused by outside interference.[22] We fight among ourselves. We attack our leaders. We place ourselves in jeopardy. There was a time when things were different for us and for the land.

A LAMENT TO WESTERN CANADA

buffalo tilled
prairie sod
till cut beneath
a foreign plow
furrows deep then deeper
from the heart of soil
to offer grain
for settlers flooding in

that railway
snaked its way
across the west
carrying soldiers
hellbent on revenge
against a people
wanting only to
survive

Canada bequeathed
her future
from fur traders to
farmers, merchantmen
and soldiers
who hold glory for their
misbegotten past
half-breeds displaced
and all because of
prairie gold
kept up the profiteers

Not only do we fight with those outside our communities, we fight within them as well.

WE ARE BOTH
We get awful huffy
when it comes to blood
I say Indian
you say white
Who hurt us?
Left us claiming
half ourselves?
Do I deny our dad
while you deny our mom?
We're neither right
not you or me
We're both
We're blended not
divided, separated
me Indian
you white
as if we could just be one
and not the other
with a French dad
and "half-breed" mother
We are both
We are Metis

We have an interesting legacy, we Metis. It pisses me off when I read scholars like Flanagan who use theory to attack our right to exist, to have "rights" like other people. If they could only live inside our heads and hearts and see us as human beings maybe, maybe, things could be different.

Who is this ghost
who haunts all of us?
Who makes children tremble
Who makes fathers cry
and mothers die?
Who is this white ghost
who came to this land
spawning new
generations?
Who is this white ghost?

Cries From A Metis Heart

Who is this Indian ghost
that together created
but now both deny
the fruits of passion
seeded in their loins
How can they sanctify
their lust without thought
for offspring thrown
amid a world of Catholic
Protestant division
Indian, white separation?
Yet we the fruit of their passion
weave the sash that binds
us all.
Half-breed,
half-burnt wood
I'm not half anything
I am, I am
Metis

Now Flanagan wants to deny us a significant part of our heritage. He claims in his 1983 article entitled *The Case Against Metis Aboriginal Land Rights* that the Canadian government made a historical mistake by granting the Red River Metis Aboriginal rights in 1870. According to Flanagan, Metis did not exist until whites came to North America. Needless to say, he is fixating on one part of Metis ancestry while totally dismissing the other half. He argues that Metis culture (food, clothing, housing and farming practices), although modified by Indians, was based on the European model. With the obviously Eurocentric bias he came to the conclusion that Metis Aboriginal rights were bogus. If he only understood what lives in our hearts. We face rejection by whites, rejection by Indians, and now when we are beginning to assert our pride in being Metis, he wants to reject us as Metis.

RED WEEDS
You couldn't understand
my pain that day as you
callously yanked the dandelions
from my yard
tearing them out of their
life blood

then justified yourself
by saying, it's just a weed.
It isn't just a matter of
pulling out the weeds
It's the idea . . . the idea
of a plant being ugly
which came with Europeans'
first visit
Ever since then the white man has tried
to destroy the freedom in our life
calling us savage – our gardens a weed
Imagine control
and structured beauty
aren't we lucky you say
you saved our lives
you gave us your blood – made us beautiful
stripped away our freedom, killed our weeds
then – set our relatives
in neat little
garden boxes – only we call them
Reservations
then calmly dismissed
the mixed blood child
But we are still like weeds
trampled, feeling your contempt
We cannot be – soft tender with
blushed pink cheeks
Ah – a rose petal won't
blossom forth from
sun-kissed brown, wilting flesh
Hyacinth blue won't shine
in empty deep-brown sockets
NO! NO!
You can't steal our beauty
You don't know
Metis
We are like the dandelion
free to roam and taste the land

Cries From A Metis Heart

We lift our battered petals
Fluff our leaves
Gather up our roots
And flee your bounded space
We're free
We're free … we are
like the weed
You cannot kill us
We are Metis

We Metis carry the stories our grandmothers told. We carry them and we survive.

SHE WALKED

She walked this earth with endless grace
her stories etched upon her face
a life lived long and hard but full

For age there is no bridge to youth
returning flesh to tender firm
her beauty lies not in youthful bloom

But in the stories she trod on earth
each wrinkled line a song of old
She floats upon my memory forever

Bearing my future
in the strength of her stride
as she walks beneath an endless sky.

People are pretty funny sometimes. They chose what they want to glamorize, sensationalize and accept.

INDIAN BE INDIAN

Indian be Indian
echoes
my heart
I dance alone
together as
we move
I sing alone
in unison.

I circle slowly
as you
glamorize my dress
my hair
Loudly whispering
"Indian she's Indian"
as soft moccasins paint
the earth
with stories ages old.

Snap, your camera
missed the voices
of my ancestors
as we
dance slowly, slowly
round the circle
"Indian be Indian"
they whisper to me
as you glamorize my dress
my hair.

While I am not an Indian in the eyes of Canada's government I do recognize my interconnectedness to my "Indian blood," although I cannot say it has always been easy or painless. There are many ways we can come to recognize our interconnectedness to our bloodlines and also to our land.

I wrote the following poem in honour of Steven DeMontigny after I had invited him to play his fiddle in my class one day. As Steven played and the music flowed so did the memories of my mother's stories about Pine Bluff, and I felt the loss my mother must have experienced when her home and friends were taken away from her. I want to thank Steven for awakening in me the respect my mother deserved. I realized too what it would have taken for my grandparents to build a solid community in the north in the aftermath of 1870-1885[23] to the loneliness and suffering that would have followed the brutality of incoming settlers, the degradation of becoming Road Allowance people[24] and the depth of perseverance that flowed in my grandparents' and great-grandparents' blood. As I learned the historical truth of my Metis ancestors' experiences I came to a deep love and respect for our history.

Cries From A Metis Heart

THE FIDDLE MAN

The fiddle man played today
and my heart sang with memory
but cried in silence when
he played an ode to his community
I felt the sadness as he played to the loss
of his community Ste. Madeleine [25]
Cleared of Metis
cleared for cows
and then I saw Pine Bluff . . . in my mind
The floodwaters looming over
the horizon
I saw the men desperate to save
their livelihood
the nets lost in the blur
of rushing anger
while mothers
quickly packed their meagre
households . . . I felt their pain
The loss of Pine Bluff
Cleared of Metis
Cleared to light the houses of the south

How many times must we
lose our homes our land
Yet never lose our hearts
The fiddle man changed tempo
and suddenly I saw
in my mind my mom tapping
her toes to the rhythm of the spoons
I saw the dancing couples
I heard the laughter
and in my mind's eye I saw
the Pine Bluff she hungered
for her entire life
the friends she was separated from
I saw my home
I saw my family

I saw my roots
I felt my Metis heritage
and I was proud ...
so proud of my ancestors
as I watched that fiddle man
tap his toes to the beat
of that wooden magic
I felt
the emotion being sung forth
as that fiddle man played
the memories of our
land

I wrote this chapter to show honour to my identity, and to show that in spite of legacies of destruction we have survived and we will continue to not only survive but also thrive, because our support comes from many areas and our storytellers come in many forms. And the stories, like those flowing from Steven's fiddle music, tell of pride, dignity and survival.

NOTES

17 The Manitoba Act of 1870 provided substantial land grants to the Metis at Red River. Section 31 of the Act set aside 1.4 million acres of land for redistribution among the children of Metis heads of families residing in the province. Section 32 guaranteed all old settlers, Metis or white, "peaceable possession" of the lots they occupied in the Red River settlement prior to July 15, 1870. Additional legislation of 1874 guaranteed $160 scrip, redeemable to Dominion lands, to all Metis heads of families. However, very little of this land and scrip remained with the Metis by the late 1870s. Through various fraudulent acts, most of that land was taken by unscrupulous land speculators. Unfortunately, there are scholars who contest the idea that Canada did not treat the Metis in a fair and equitable manner regarding the subsequent land scrip distribution. The most notable adversary is Thomas Flanagan, a political scientist from the University of Calgary and a historical consultant for the federal Department of Justice. Flanagan generally takes the view that the government acted in good faith, and honorably discharged all its obligations to the Metis.

18 After the 1982 Canadian Constitution accepted Metis people as one of the Aboriginal peoples of Canada, Flanagan contests the very idea of Metis people being Aboriginal. See his article, "The Case Against Metis Aboriginal Rights," Vol. 9, No. 3 (Sept., 1983, pp. 314-325) where he argues that, "Metis aboriginal rights are a historical mistake, conceived out of political expediency in 1870 to pacify the insurgents in Red River." He goes on to argue that "the best strategy to minimize the damage caused by the thoughtless elevation of the Metis to the status of a distinct 'aboriginal' people is to emphasize the word, 'existing,' in sections 35 of the Charter of Rights and Freedoms."

19 A popular method the Canadian government used for distributing land in the 1800s was through issuing scrip, either land or money scrip. Scrip looked like money and

often came in dollar amounts, but neither money scrip nor land scrip was really money in the strict sense of the word. The only real value it had was that it could be exchanged or redeemed for a certain amount of Dominion land from the government. Money scrip was seen as personal property and could be sold easily. Land scrip, however, was seen as real estate and could be redeemed only by the person named on the scrip, though it would not be too difficult to find someone willing to pretend to be the person named in the scrip and to forge a signature.

[20] In our advanced age of technology we have people using the Internet to discredit other Metis people by throwing out ugly innuendos designed to destroy someone's credibility in what is commonly known as character assassination.

[21] See the book: *Rotten to the Core: The Politics of the Manitoba Metis Federation*, published in 1995. The author, Sheila Jones Morrison, detailed the development of the Manitoba Metis Federation. The author used every instance in the history of the development and most of its leaders to discredit Metis people and their struggle to obtain political and cultural recognition.

[22] The divide-and-conquer tactic is an ancient strategy used to keep people fighting. Governments are able to offer substantial funding, but the funding often leads us into suspicion of either government motives or our own leaders' motives. When we do not know whom to trust we are open to manipulation by friends and family who cry nepotism, fraud and theft when things are do not go the way they would like, and then cheering unity, Metis pride and so forth when things are going the way they would like. Sometimes it seems like obtaining more funding is more important than cultural unity.

[23] After the 1870 resistance in Manitoba and the second one in 1885 in Saskatchewan, Metis people found themselves in a very difficult position. They were economically, politically and personally persecuted by incoming settlers and government. Many families moved north, south or west in the hope of finding a new home. My own grandparents moved north, leaving their families, friends and way of life behind. They began a new life, but it must have been difficult to leave behind all they had known.

[24] Many Metis people found themselves homeless and they became squatters, living on land that they did not even own. From 1885-1945, the landless Metis moved from locale to locale, often under force, in order to make a living and live among themselves. Towns set aside land designated for future roads, and homeless Metis were often found living on those allotments. They became known as Road Allowance people. These Metis had a difficult time finding suitable housing for themselves in the face of extensive non-Aboriginal settlement on the Prairies. Therefore, road allowance houses were usually tarpaper shacks built from discarded lumber or logs. Since Road Allowance people did not pay taxes they were often excluded from communities and many of their children were denied access to public schools.

[25] In the late 1930s the Metis community of Ste. Madeleine, Man. was relocated in the name of development. Some say their community was taken to feed cows.

Red River Jig
6

When I was a little girl I loved listening to the fiddle. My favorite music was the Red River Jig. I would tap my toes anxiously till one day I finally learned how to jig. For me jigging is a source of pure joy and reflects pride in my Metis heritage. It is for this reason that I chose to title this section Red River Jig. I have danced many steps through my life in an effort to survive. I began this work with the title, *Cries from a Metis Heart*, because I wanted to show the depth of pain some of us carry and to speak from my heart. I am also no longer willing to sleep with victimization as my life's partner. All my writing has helped clarify my history, what I carried and how it impacted me. The process of writing it has helped me recognize that I am an amazing woman. I am a survivor, I have strength, as have every other Metis woman, man and child. There are many poems and stories contained in this book that were painful to write, but to tell them was to break the silence and that is the beginning to healing.

THE MASK
The sun will rise in an hour
One more step
One more day
One more mask
to put in place

The bus comes in a minute
One more ride
One more day
The academic mask
must not fall down

Almost there
Begin to smile
lest they see your fear
The mask of assurance
must never slip

Almost over
Take a breath
Unlock the office door
The mask in place
step outside

The bus comes in a minute
Another day is done
A new mask
must fall in place
A mask of family love

The sun has gone
the night creeps in
It's bedtime now
no mask is needed
just a face no one has seen

Not only did I carry an ever-present mask, but also I struggled with uncertainty of belonging. This is not unusual for a mixed blood child. I began my stories with one of my aunt and knowing her love came with deceit. How could it not when she complained so bitterly about her brothers marrying half-breeds and I knew my mom was a half-breed? The bitterness that followed her words and haunted me throughout my life had to be resolved. I had to overcome her rejection and every other person's rejection. Part of that overcoming was recognizing and dealing with the rage that came from rejection of my bloodlines.

FAKE COPY
Who I am – is not who you think
living in the dark shadows
hidden from your light

Buried in deep recesses – of the mind
lives a soul – longing
for recognition – but

alone, afraid – afraid
to come out and
face your world

the crushing weight keeps
pushing, driving, hurting
alone, spinning out of control

a girl weeps for a life
that never was – dreaming
of something never experienced

denied by her beige flesh
a watered version
a fake copy

KEEP OUT
There is no one home for her

I guess I lived as a fake copy to many others besides myself. There are First Nations people today who still reject my Cree side and Canadians who reject my French side. Some want to call me "white" and others call me "Indian," and some still say "half-breed". So it is no wonder I felt like a fake copy. But in truth I am not a fake anything. I am a Metis woman. I am a Metis woman who had to come home in the sense of trusting herself to be who she is, Metis. Only in this way could I rise above the bitterness of wanting to be what I am not and trying to be what I could not be and pleading for someone to accept me.

LOVE WITHOUT LUST
You entered my world of suspicion
bringing friendship that I never knew
could exist without releasing my body
to a mind without soul
I knew how to hate and mistrust
I knew how to hide in the night
from hands grasping an
innocent child
I learned that there is no
safety for a girl child
in a world controlled by men
But
you came into my world of suspicion
brought friendship without any strings
You taught me to let you love me

a love without lust on your part
At first I was frightened, so frightened
Your gentleness feeling so strange
Your eyes being fully sincere
your hands never grasping
ignoring my terrible fear
To think that someone
could love me without
first consuming my soul
demanding *his* right to my body
To think that me, just me
was good enough
Good enough to be loved without lust
I learned that there could be safety
for a woman still child
and
that I am worth being loved
being loved without lust

I found it interesting when I wrote the above poem. For above all else it revealed how much I had come to accept that "love" was nothing more than a sexual encounter. I had so much to overcome, and to finally find a friend who cared simply because I was Lorraine astounded me. I kept questioning his friendship as if waiting to be betrayed. Betrayal never arrived. Instead, I saw betrayal from other areas. Movies, books and toys taught female children how to look, to feel, to love; indeed they taught everything we needed to know about our existence. There is our true betrayal, all nicely packaged in fantasy fiction.

I am fighting back now. I am not simply sitting taking what life throws at me. I am fighting back. I am seeing beyond the pain and anguish that kept me blinded for too long. I see there are ways to confront the past while healing the present. I am finally beginning to see me.

I see the haunting pain
behind your smile
Walk away – don't run
your tears won't hide
his vicious theft
You're worth the world to us
Shame need not fill your footsteps

Give wings to guilt
It was never you
Turn the on page on memory
longing for what never was
trapped by his rape
questioning – always
what could and should have been
only tightens the chains
around your heart
Be free and fly
away from his vile theft
The world is waiting for you
to release your history – to the wind
and fly free – to be
the woman you were meant to be

I started to see where my power came from and what I could do with it. I also realized that at moments of absolute weakness I was never truly alone, for women long gone guided me. They provided me with their strength so I could go another mile. I did not know these women, but I treasure the strength they passed on to me.

When I began to see myself as other than a frightened little girl I began to look out to the world and I saw myself and my life in a different context. The pain of my life had so overwhelmed my senses that I missed seeing the support that had been there. I have not done all this myself. I am not an island. I had people; I just could not see them, I could not feel them and most of all I could not trust them. Nonetheless, they were always there.

My mother, my grandmother and great-grandmothers have always been here for me in ways I could not see. They had passed on lessons I needed to survive, but did not realize were lessons. There were also women not related to me who played important roles in my life. My parents had placed me in Catholic school for a few years, and in that time I met nuns, most of whom I did not trust or even like. One stayed with me, and she was also an unknown source of strength.

SISTER ADELARD

Sister Adelard
told me buffalo
roamed where I played
Could she be that old?
Sister Conrad said
I had the makings of a nun
Could she be that blind?
I hated that black dress
and weird wedding veil
But I didn't hate
Sister Adelard

Once I realized how many beautiful people had been discarded by my blindness and my fear of letting anyone get close to me I began a mission of trying to tell people what happened, to break the silence. I saw that I was not the only woman to live in isolated fear. I wanted others to hear what we as abused Metis women feel like. I wanted people to see beyond my masks.

APOLOGY?

I was a movie star once
Me, my class, and my crocus
I took that flower to
school, I only wanted to
give it to my teacher
They brought the TV cameras
to document the first
Crocus of the season
I was famous for a while
Everyone was thrilled to see
my Manitoba crocus
So I stood there shyly holding
out the crocus. My prize
that put me on TV
My crocus?
I never told them
You should have been
the movie star It
should have been your class

Cries From A Metis Heart

we watched that night
on the six o'clock news.
You found that stupid flower
but I never told the truth

It is a funny thing how much guilt an adult woman can cling to over a child-hood escapade. But the truth is I had learned to remain silent in everything. The guilt over the little lie of omission has remained a constant companion, and I hope one day to sit with my sister and laugh about the day she gave me that flower instead of seeing that flower as a reminder of my ugliness.

There are so many ways I hurt myself and denied myself that I wondered if I could ever change. I always sought out advice, terrified to make the wrong choice because I might be punished. I did not trust myself or my ability to think clearly. I moulded myself after what I thought others wanted me to be . . .

Yet, the answers have always been inside of me, but I did not trust my-self to know anything. I moulded myself after what I thought others wanted me to be. I dressed to please others. I acted in ways that would please others. Paradoxically, while I made myself visible to others, I made myself invisible to myself and ultimately I was really invisible to others. When I began to do things for myself I was surprised at how it made me feel. I was also surprised at what becoming visible did to others and my reaction to their reaction. For example, I love to wear the colour pink, yet there was a time I would not be caught wearing it, simply because I heard feminists criticizing people for putting their little girls in pink. They called it socializing daughters into a gendered picture of the world where boys wear blue and girls wear pink. The feminists I knew were staunchly opposed to the wearing of pink, so of course I quit wearing pink. I did not want to be ridiculed. Then one day I bought a pink jacket and many other pieces of pink clothing.

PINK
identified gendered
colour – pink.
I have a few pieces
of pink in my wardrobe
I have many black
blazers and suit jackets
I wear on a continual basis
noticing. I get neither
compliments nor

condemnation when
dressed this way.
I simply am.
I am not present.
On the other hand
on those days when
I choose to wear pink
I am befuddled. I get
many comments heavy
with condemnation or
laced with subtle criticism.
Occasionally
I hear "you wear pink?"
as if I had just arrived
from Mars.
Other times
"ooh, you look good in pink."
What I have come to appreciate
is that in wearing pink
I have become visible
I am present.

Imagine my surprise at discovering that I had made myself visible. After years of consciously presenting a non-presence I now wanted to be seen and I was rejecting the notion that others could make me a non-presence. I was also recovering that which I lost as a child, faith in myself and in my choices. I was finally asserting my own right to choose for myself what I wear, what I think and where I go. I was taking back my life. Once I purged myself of the guilt and shame of my past I began to see with different eyes.

FOR MY GRANDCHILDREN
I heard your voices
and my heart soars
to the moon
I am in wonderment
that soft tones can
set my heart on fire
How did you come
into my life and

Cries From A Metis Heart

alter my dependency
on only me?

I see your smiles and
my body wants to dance
across the green
I am in amazement
that tiny grins
can be felt
within another's body
How did you come
into my life and
alter my sadness
for everything?
My grandchildren how
did you weave
this magic?

Eventually I came to realize that what has been robbed from us as mixed blood children who have experienced racial discrimination, cultural rejection and abusive homes is the ability to have intimate relationships, whether with the opposite sex or the same sex or ourselves. With intimacy we have trust. Without trust we are alone, and when alone we make our own conclusions about life. We need others to help us see that the world is not just a place of violence. We need others to help us learn that violence is not normal. We need friends, lovers and community. We are social animals and were never meant to be alone. We are human beings who deserve to be loved. We are people who have the right to exist in safety.

INTIMACY: FOR MY FRIEND
Too late in life
I crossed your path
to be the woman
in your arms.
Yet, friendship
forged a stronger link
binding our stories into one
Intimacy is my friend
whose eyes reflected
a past unknown

whose laughter healed
the pain within.
Intimacy is my friend
as we walk together
in harmony
balancing each other's faults
returning over and over
to a place we must
have walked a hundred
years ago
emptying one heart into the another
revealing deepest trauma
locked far away in souls
untouched.
Tread lightly intimacy
lest we shatter
this fragile mirror
reflecting back our existence
as we place trust
in each other's eyes
and draw strength from
each other's lives
We opened hearts
and intimacy came in
to tie the knot
of friendship
carved in unity.
I crossed your path
and not too late
You crossed my path
and just in time
to restore
a faith in intimacy.

I am learning to have faith in things like intimacy. There is a closeness, a sense of togetherness, a belonging that comes with intimacy that had been lacking in my life. I began this section talking about the Red River Jig because for me it has always been a source of strength. The Metis fiddle player has always been a hero to me. Today our fiddlers continue to make magic. We as Metis people are also making magic. I am learning to dance a new dance, one filled with pure joy. The magic of words has healed me in ways I never thought possible. I once read that "the truth will set you free, but first it will make you miserable." Writing the truth of my life in my poems and stories has done exactly that; it has made me miserable, but it has also set me free.

MY HEROES ARE NOT

My heroes are not
on Wall Street, they
never were.
My heroes walked
through Tobique,
through The Pas,
down the halls of the
McLaren Hotel.
They stagger past
white leches,
condemning white
women,
judgmental teachers,
arrogant social workers,
humiliating white
legislation
government elites,
fancy cars and houses.
My heroes walked past
all these obstacles and
surfaced fully human.
They may be drunk,
stoned and alone but
they are alive,
damn it
they are alive.
They live and breathe
the foul air of
racism
yet they surface again
and again, always

reminding me that
the world is full of
hypocrisy and
self-hatred
so deep most outsiders
not to mention the
insider herself
cannot recognize
the depth
of its destruction.
I cry, partly from
helplessness,
partly from rage
but mostly
from a deep sense of
injustice
I have nothing to
offer these women
but my pen and my anger
and my respect

I had always kept my poems hidden away so no one could read my deepest thoughts. Then one day I shared some with a close friend and that beginning spiraled out of control and resulted in this book. With the help of others who believed in me and what I wrote I took the challenge to write this book. It is my deepest hope that my words will help set someone else free.

My Symposium

7

I've come a long way since I first began writing my pain in what I call my poetry. I've confronted my own demons. I've looked at myself as a woman, with the multiple violations I experienced and my own personal failings. I have looked at my culture and who I am as a Metis. I've looked at my Metis history and found pride. Yet there is one more area that is intimately interconnected to my past that has changed my life in ways I never thought possible. As I said, as I learned the historical truth of my Metis ancestors' experiences I came to a deep love and respect for our history. I was able to do this in large part because of the formal education I received at university. My education has provided me with the opportunity to learn the truth of Metis people, to see beyond the misrepresentations to see honour instead of shame. Today I teach a course titled *The Metis* at university, and each time I teach this class I am filled with gratitude and hope for the future of other students.

My education has done a lot for me, and there were so many struggles to endure and so many times I just wanted to run and give up that I decided I must also tell this story. I must for all those students who like me want to give up in the face of racist[27] and discriminatory obstacles and our own low self-esteem.

To begin with, getting a degree was in and of itself an amazingly difficult process, but to continue with a PhD program almost seemed impossible. The choice to continue was made more difficult by the fact that the only school I could get into was in the United States. It took tremendous courage to walk away from my family, my home and my country to complete my education. Without this courage and strength I would not have a new legacy to pass to my children and grandchildren. I wrote a letter to my daughter while I was living in Oregon because I needed her to hear me, hear what I have kept silent for so long. I wanted to bequeath her a new story. And so I'd like to share my letter:

A LETTER FOR DANIELLE

I write this letter to you because I needed you to know why I struggled and why I wouldn't give up. Mostly however, I have wanted you to know how close you are to my heart and I believe you can have happiness and sense of self-respect in spite of our historical legacy of oppression, pain and disillusionment. Every day that I struggled to complete a PhD in philosophy not a day went by that I didn't think of our family back in Canada. I constantly questioned my sanity in traveling halfway across North America, leaving my family and friends behind, sacrificing our happiness together for a dream that might in reality have been an illusion.

You are a grown woman now. Somehow my little girl has blossomed into a woman with her own children, and so much of that time I have not been with you. I remember the day you had your first baby, I cried in joy but I also cried for our loss. The loss of a mother not being present to share in the wonderment of her daughter's first birthing. I think often of not sharing Austin's birth. I had dreamed for years about us being together when you gave birth for the first time. I thought I would be there to help you get through, to laugh with you, to cry with you and to show you how proud I am of you. Instead, the ringing of a telephone in the wee hours announced his imminent arrival.

I know you are proud of your mother and what I was trying to accomplish. But, sometimes I doubted my strength to carry our plans. I missed you so much, and when the loneliness overwhelmed me I would become terrified that I would quit and that I would let you down and then the sacrifices we have had to go through for this education would have been for nothing. All those years of intensive study that kept me from you. All the times you had to amuse yourself because I was too busy with my books. I still laugh when I think of how we tried to compensate for lost time together. Do you remember how you and your brothers would read passages from my books for me so I could cook dinner or wash the dishes? Remember how your brother teased me about having the name "Bishop George Berkley" permanently imprinted in his mind, and how you struggled to say "Sigmund Freud?"

I know you say I did not neglect you, but I felt the palpable effects of my neglect each day as I watched you grow out of childhood into young womanhood and I realized how much of your life, your joys, and your girlish secrets I have missed. I always knew I could not provide you with the things you needed to make a young teen's life more tolerable. I promised myself I would make it better for you. When my educational experiences became overwhelming, when the racism cut deep and when the hypocrisy seemed insurmountable, I knew I could not walk away from the disillusionment and pain. I could not; otherwise all the shared time we have lost through the years would have made your sacrifices meaningless. I could not do this to you, to your brothers and to myself and I could not do this to our future.

Yet, how often, I wondered, did the thoughts of non-Aboriginal students center on painful self-doubt? Do other students question the validity of their own existence?

Cries From A Metis Heart

Do other students question their identity, their place of belonging? Do they? Do they feel the intense sadness, the helpless bitterness that so overwhelms each time we are confronted with scholarly hypocrisy?[29] Do they know the rage that boils our blood, do they? Or how much we must sacrifice in order to complete these degrees?[30]

SOCRATES WHAT HAPPENED

Socrates what happened
to me that day
I heard your words
at school?
I felt myself drawn to
your cave wanting only to
follow you down
that winding
path in search of
knowledge.
Now I swim a
morass
of lethargy in
thought wondering
how it could come to be
that my thoughts keep
spiraling out of
control.
My inner thoughts I
once enjoyed I now call
fantasy.
I flounder around
befuddled by the
experiences of daily life.
Did you know I listened
to René Descartes?
Oh yes I did.
He taught me how to doubt
Now too often I find I am
suspicious of everyone's
motivations
wondering if they doubt me
like I doubt them.

Socrates, I once knew where
to step, confident
in my ability to reason.
Now I stagger in
confusion

Thought I knew who I was
now I wonder
Socrates what happened?

How confused could I be? How confused can you be? I went to Oregon to learn philosophy. I had a love of wisdom, a joy to learn and a desire to share our world, our philosophy, yet I found so many contradictions. Philosophers write about justice, but how can I believe in justice when all around me I see injustice? Where is the injustice philosophers talk about when in North America scholars, government officials and religious practitioners steal our very being without a flicker of an eye? Where is justice when they condemn our hunt, yet their food intoxicates the bloodline of our heritage, leaving a legacy of diabetes? Where is justice when non-native people let us be Indians in regalia full, but deny or ignore the values that flow within our veins? Where is the justice when they destroy the lifeblood on this planet and then impose their cultural values to dictate the standards of our beliefs and practices?[31] Where is the justice when I challenge their notions of justice and am told to "be fair?" Justice, where is their justice? I am sure Socrates never intended hypocrisy to be the foundation for justice.

Philosophy deals with questions of reality, but philosophers from the Americas seem to be geographically blind. They do not seem to see the philosophies from other nations. I have been long interested in how people understand their worlds and it has become clear to me that while many people share different beliefs it is only the Western European-descended philosophers that are blind to the limitations of their philosophy. From the beginning of written philosophy with the Greeks, philosophy was known as the "Love of Wisdom." A genuine love of wisdom should eagerly embrace the realities of other cultures. But the last century has succinctly shown me that contemporary philosophy would be best identified as "The Love of Western Wisdom." If whatever wisdom we have does not come from their lips or their pens, then it must not be wisdom. Other interpretations of reality are too often reduced to mere rhetoric or paganism. Even when acknowledged, the wisdoms of other peoples must take a back seat to the Western world until an intellect decides to appropriate it, then it becomes theirs and is no longer primitive or dogma – it becomes wisdom.

It is ironic how academics enjoy parading the euphemism, "we don't live in an ancient world," to deny the validity of alternative thinking when they themselves

Cries From A Metis Heart

are locked into the "timeless" truths of dead white men. Yet, when confronted with ancient, non-European-descended wisdom they balk and spew their jargon, possibly hoping we will forget, transcend their theft and genocide and walk humbly behind, grateful for any philosophical considerations they may toss about. On the other hand, while it is true that contemporary philosophers do not physically live in an ancient world, many Native American thinkers do. Ancient, that is, if one considers that the value placed in difference and the ultimate value of life, connection and relationships is centuries old and still operative today. Then yes, many Native Americans still live in an ancient world. This is not to say we physically live in an ancient world; the noble savage is their myth, not ours. Nor do we do nothing but pine for a return to our ancient ways, though we do grieve for them. Yes, we live in this modern world with all its accompanying amenities, but we live an ancient morality that is as appropriate today as it was centuries ago.

Western thinkers think they have evolved their philosophical tradition from the ancient Greeks' love of wisdom to what we know of the contemporary epistemological search for knowledge, the metaphysical search for what is really real and an ethical search for the best possible moral theory. They applaud the brilliance of their rational thought, calling other cultural interpretations of reality, knowledge, and ethics, primitive or superstitious. I am fascinated with the egos that blind them to the truth of their progression – a progression founded on theft, deceit and paternalism. Many Western thinkers do not even value the wisdom of their own females. How, then, can I expect them to value a woman from both inside and outside the western tradition?

We live at a time of serious cultural problems with imperialist, paternalist, and relativist understandings competing with each other. Racism, discrimination, sexism, and elitism are some of the effects resulting from these three conceptualizations. The longer I walked the academic path the angrier I would get. However, the angrier I got the more my reason for being here revealed itself to me. I must pick up my pen and do battle. I must claim a warrior's courage. I must demand an academic place to be heard, I must or my grandson will blossom in a world not of our making. I write for my children, for my grandchildren, for our ancestors, and today for kakinowniwako-makinuk.[32]

I do not want my grandson to grow in a world that holds no value for his blood, a world that denies his existence, a world that values only his maleness, a world that places him above his mother, his grandmother and his great-grandmother. I want him to know his roots, his present, and his future. I want him to be proud of his Cree blood. I want him to know his culture is vibrant. I want him to know his responsibilities as a male child. I want him to know the sacredness of his birth and his mother's deepest *love and commitment. I want him to know the philosophy of his heritage and not the misconceptions of a twisted reality enforced upon him by a world that holds no honesty and no dignity. I want him to know the importance of strength, determination, courage and love.*

I could have told him all these things without the pain of North American education, but then I would not be showing him how to become a warrior to survive in this world. I would not be teaching him how to become a silent hero. I would not be bringing the story to life for him. We have always been a people with stories, but we did not simply sit around regaling each other with empty stories. No, not at all! The stories were of instances of action; an action that the storyteller and the whole community would live and responded to with action. Long ago when I wanted to learn how to make bannock my mother said, "Watch me." Education for me is like my mother's modeling procedure. I cannot shape my grandson, nor would I want to, but I can provide him with the opportunity to watch the story grow. I can provide him with an alternative picture of women and Aboriginal people, a picture unlike the ones that are still too popular in media and education.

Philosophy was my chosen vehicle, and regardless of how bad it gets or maybe because of how bad it gets, philosophy is still my chosen vehicle With it I can ride the roughest terrain. Indeed, any Aboriginal traveling an academic journey is continually confronted with obstacles not of our making.[33] Many roads need careful negotiating, some detours will be necessary and sometimes we need to cancel a particular trip for a short period. Nonetheless, we will not be roadblocked – sideswiped, maybe, but no longer prohibited from beginning the journey.

PHILOSOPHER QUEEN

Philosopher king
how does it feel
to meet a
philosopher queen?
She walks through halls
wrapped in your words
She may stumble and fall
but she never gives in
for her strength is built
on her ancestor's words
Someday she'll walk
the path you forged
till then she'll work

with the strength of a
Grandfather long gone
She'll live with the
words of courage
her Grandmother
bequeathed to
soften the blows
that say she does not
belong
Philosopher Queen
walks steadily on
weaving the truth from
a distortion of years

When our grandchildren want to enter the upper echelons of academia we need people there who will guide them, offer support and show them it can be done! When I look back at how hard it was to complete my education I also think of all the rewards. I have met many wonderful people who have supported me throughout this entire adventure. I have met (through their writings) many strong Aboriginal women and men who have unknowingly guided me through the years of loneliness and fear. They provided the necessary role models to help me see past the institutions of bigotry. They helped me recognize that I am not alone and have never been alone. These courageous scholars provided the support that helped me regain my own sense of dignity and inspired me to pass on more than alienation to my children and grandchildren.

As for philosophy, I still see it as the search for truth, not the absolute, universalistic truth sought after by so many others. No, my truth is a truth about our history, our philosophy, our ways of knowing and doing.

MY SYMPOSIUM
I fell onto the couch that graced the symposium
and lost myself to dreams.
I walked a beaten path
to feel the Parthenon
I heard the voice of
ancient philosophers
and felt the mystery.
Oh Socrates, oh Plato
Your words remain
Embedded in the minds of

Womenfolk left behind.
Left trying to make sense
To recreate a world created
through simplicity in words
by philosophers confused.
Why Socrates, why Plato
you saw your strength
in understanding ... all.
You saw not the beauty
that unfolds the starlit night
breathing serenity
upon the land.
You saw quadrangles with
mathematical certainty
and forced the absolute out of
fluidity denying the source
of life pulsating change.
then asked what's really real.
You saw not the life
in women's hands but
only warrior's skills
holding aloft a deadly sword
and hailed the mighty man
But you missed the mother's
strength that brought him out
of the womb to manly time
Oh Socrates, oh Plato
You saw the politics
the fair republic held aloft
You heard not the voice
that soothed the turbulent
trials of hunger, chaos, fear
that winds its way through
families long before the man
has learned to crawl out of
reality into metaphysical
confusion ... placing man above
it all.

Cries From A Metis Heart

At my symposium
I saw the candles burning
I smelled the sweetgrass
I saw my grandmother
Walking

My truth is about the opportunity to develop the skills necessary to give honour to the people whose struggles paved the way for my being in academia. I cannot let myself forget where I come from and why. I realize I am here and I struggle because I do see injustice and I will continue to address the injustice with every fibre of my being.

I struggled because I am a mother, a grandmother, a daughter, a friend and a relative. I struggled because I have a responsibility to my family to help us see a way out of the quagmire we were rapidly sinking into. I struggled because I believe in Aboriginal people and I know we are capable of resurfacing from lives of pain, disillusionment and racism into a life where we can be respected, a life we will help to create. I struggled to complete this education because I believe in the strength of our heritage, I believe in the courage it takes to walk every day amid discrimination and racism. And, mostly I struggled because I believe in our future.

Today I realize I had focused so much of my attention on what we have sacrificed by my journey through education that I nearly missed the most important lesson a mother can pass on to her daughter. I forgot that perseverance and the refusal to be beaten up or beaten down were silent lessons you were absorbing. I almost forgot that seeing your mother rise above abject poverty, abuse and self-destruction were crucial lessons for a young woman embarking on her own life. I may not have been there as much as I would have liked, but because of my choices you now have choices and there is no better gift a mother can pass on to her daughter.

No, I could not be with you when you birthed your first child, but I want you to know that I was with you in spirit and I want to give you something tangible to pass on to your son. I wrote this poem for my mother and it attests to the freedom of my spirit, a gift I received from my education. Not the formal education of the system, but the education of experience and survival that I learned from both my mother and my own struggles to complete a formal education. This gift of freedom has for too long been denied to our family and it is this gift I would like to pass on to your children and to your nieces and nephews.

MAMA DON'T CRY FOR ME

My great-grandfather was a buffalo hunter
The Government said he was a redskin
My grandfather was a trapper
The Government called him a half-breed
My mama was a housemaid
The Government said she was white
And me, my ma mère, pa père were French
So now the Government calls me Metis
Who were they to dictate who you were?
Tearing red roots from their soil
Forming with each generation a brand new Breed
Each step up, a bloodline down
Another statistic lost in the wind

They forced another world into your flesh
Until you hung your head in shame
Hidden away from who you are
Speaking someone else's foreign tongue
The path I chose made you afraid
But, don't cry for me mama
'Cause I know who I am
Just take my hand mama
Look deep within your heart
And stay close by my side –
I have the strength to fight them back now
Mama – I have the strength

It's our time now, to live our ancestry
We can restore your Indian pride
I reached into our history to
Find red roots wilted in their soil
Submersed in the world confused
Rejected, but never completely forgotten
'Cause my great-grandmother
Cooked the buffalo
My grandmother cooked the muskrat
You may have hid the bannock
while ma mère fed me her beef
But I know who I am

Because . . .
I come from a culture of genocide
I come from a culture of pride
I carry two distinct bloodlines
The government no longer denies
My memory lives in two distinct homes
The city of Winnipeg The Pas in the north
I think with two distinct educations
One traditional Cree passed down
Through hundreds of years
The other a Western tradition
A recent phenomenon here

But, I know who I am
'Cause my great-grandfather
Was a buffalo hunter
And my grandfather was a trapper
I carry them mama
In my heart along with
buffalo pounding in my head
And muskrats swimming in my veins
Yes. I walk in two distinct worlds
So don't cry for me mama
Don't cry

All my love, Mom

I heard a song once that talked about not having to cry forever, and I doubted its truth. Today I think differently. I do not think I will spend the rest of my life crying. I have hope for a better future. I have seen great change in my life, in my attitudes and in my actions. Today I can pay my bills without having to fear the ring of the telephone. Today I do not have to hide or walk down back lanes. Today I can laugh and today I can dream. I want this to be my legacy – laughter, dreams and love.

FOR AUSTIN
I stumble out of
the fog of pain too

glazed to see love
unfolding firm.

I love you Grandma
Tiny solemn eyes
Beseech mine to see
to hear the words
that melt my heart.

His arms as they
reach to hug and give
comfort to the woman
who birthed his mother
as she grieves her life.

I raise above the
world as his words
penetrate the deep
and I love again.

Not only have I learned what it means to laugh, dream and love. I have
learned to recall happy times. I have been able to see past the fog of pain. No life
can contain only despair, but the hurt pushed out the good. Today I am seeing
places of joy. Places that unknowingly sustained me. One especially warm memory comes from a year I spent living in St. Ambrose. To be able to remember the
good times past is a beginning to creating new ones today.

A YEAR AT ST. AMBROSE
I smelled the frost
And I remembered

Wood smoke mixed
with laughter
weathered the walls

Beds lined the length
safe in every aisle
without partitions

to hide our sleepless dreams
I remembered ...

Cries From A Metis Heart

Verna Donald Davy
you were my friends
sharing secrets in the bush

These days when night
breathes a certain chill
your faces return

As I smell the frost
I remember
Was I only 16?

hiding dishes
underneath the bed
when time called to play

My mind
returns to
cream separating

saskatoon berries
6:00 am garden theft
cows to call home

sloughs to skirt
horses to feed
I'd laugh

but complain
when the bus
arrived

taking us on journey
the long long rides
to St. Laurent

whispering secrets
passing little towns
reading, arguing, being

Lorraine Mayer

I remember St. Francis
Oak Point
The schoolyard

Ducharmes, Bruces, Lavallees
Chartrands, Allards and Dumonts
waiting patiently

for a bell to call
assembly into rooms
partitioned against

curious eyes
as Sisters read the roll
but we see anyway

I remember dances
too far from home
still you'd let us go

Gumboots, manure
chickens, I
loved your farm

But most I loved
St. Ambrose and
Aunty Edna

Your lake, your air
your dusty roads
your people

How could one year
steal my sleep
when a certain frost

is smelled
in the evening air
and I start to remember …

St. Ambrose

My eldest sister told me she was proud of me and what I had accomplished. She said she had only one request: she wanted me to write about her Reserve. She said, "people always write bad things about Indians. They never have anything good to say. But I want you to use your education to tell our story the way we see our communities." Similarly, I had believed there was nothing good in my life, but I was wrong; my perceptions were distorted. So too many people are wrong about First Nations communities, believing them to be places of only discontent, places needing relocation and places of abject despair. While there are some elements of truth in such thinking there is also the other story, the story most outsiders never see. So I wrote this next one for Easterville and for my eldest sister.

IT AIN'T ONLY BAD
There is a stillness all around
As I stare at old worn-out
Photographs hanging on my walls
Giving life to people long ago
My thoughts travel back to
The flood, relocation and confusion

Scholars document the devastation
The pain, the violence, destitution
But it ain't only bad
There is still laughter, camaraderie
A shared togetherness
That binds the people at Easterville

Children roam at will
Reveling in freedom
Swimming, teasing, alive
Grownups still recall the days
Of hunting, trapping, and the child
But memories are not simply locked in time

They surface in the present intertwined
With the changing tide of life
Amid the new is strength renewed
Daily from the past that remains present
Continuing to live in values, deeds and living
It ain't all bad. I saw the storm raging violet

Lorraine Mayer

Upon the lake where men were fishing still
We raced down to the dock
Shock froze our minds as we heard the news
My nephews were at the mercy of the elements
With no radio to reassure

The community came together
Religious differences supporting
The fear gnawing in a mother's stomach
As prayers were offered, it mattered not to whom
They came in ever increasing numbers
To stand and wait and hope.

Seasoned fishermen offered solace
when hearing who was caught out on the lake
"oh eh they are good fishermen"
"they know the lake"
"they know what to do"
no superfluous conversations
just honest sympathy
I watched in stillness as search parties
Readied for a break in wind's fierceness

Drawn faces surrounded me as
Tension mounted with children's laughter
Worked to create an understanding
Of timelessness
And, I felt the invisible pull
Of surviving as one

It ain't only bad
I remember Treaty Days
And my grandson yelling excitedly
"Kokum Jack, grandma, Kokum Jack"
as each canoe came in sight
bearing trophies small and large.

And women's merriment as men
Showed off their hairy legs and arms
With exaggerated strutting

Knowing they were nearly hairless
Unabashedly demanding to have
Their few hairs count as hairiest.

Laughter, teasing everywhere
From youngest to eldest, no one
Is saved from the torment of jest
Each equally able to return it
No offence taken none intended
No it ain't all bad.

Age holds no barrier for fun
No inhibition for play
As older women run the races
Cheekily outdistancing others
While cheering crowds yell support
Amid uproarious laughter

A community that puts a hold
On celebration to honour a
Family in mourning
This community remains
Connected to each other
In ways colonialism cannot disrupt

Heroes fighting fires
Teachers upholding Cree
Gossip at the nursing station, endless trips to The Pas
Weddings, funerals, graduations
Trees nodding agreement

No it ain't all bad
As men share the fruits of hunting, fishing
And grandmothers instruct grandchildren

Where everyone has time for a story
While new stories are created
From the adventures of new tricksters

A young princess candidate
Proudly accepts a bouquet then

Slowly walks to the elder
Sitting quietly in her wheelchair
And re-presents the bouquet
A new story of respect is birthed

The two men survived the storm
Astonished and embarrassed
At the concern they caused
Smiling sheepishly they dock their boat
And a new story of courage
And heroism is birthed

A young child learns to work
With her hands skillfully
Threading needles and beads
Eagerly leaning into her auntie's stories
And an old story is renewed and
Birthed again in the presence of a child.

No it ain't all bad.

Rather than seeing pain and ugliness all around I am beginning to see the possibility of beauty. As my perceptions are changing I find I am in love with life.

The sun shone
on Lake Michigan
and my heart
sang
for the bluest
green
I'd ever seen
I let the wind
take me back
to the days of
Al Capone
before the city
grew beyond
the shores of
Lake Michigan
and I laughed

to see the water
still remains.

I have also come to appreciate my teachers, parents, grandparents
and professors.

I dreamed you died
and I cried
I haven't seen you
in a long long time
I miss the talks the
energy you sparked
My teacher
you gave your all.
we shared stories
Laughter . . . tears
You helped my strength
take root
my dreams spread branches
and I soared to heights
determination to succeed
I was learning to live

I don't want to leave without expressing my thoughts about the men in my
culture. I know I discussed the feeling we Metis women experience when they
reject us, but they don't all reject. Some of them love us, a lot of them respect
us and a whole lot more dance life with us. This is especially true for my oldest
brother, who inspired the following poems.

DANCING LIFE
The fiddle begins to rise
nearer, nearer
to his shoulder
and a hush
fills
the expectant room
as shy gazes
search out partners.
The dance begins

in a twirl of skirts
and tapping toes
hand to hand
round and round
connecting
reconnecting
with laughter
when dark sparkling
beauty comes together.

THE BUSH

I walked the bush
picking puckons
and you laughed
to see this Metis
woman in her glory.
I stumbled through
the brush
pushing nettles
from my face
in search of
luscious
berries for my jam
cranberry, chokecherry
to cover my
le bang

HEY METIS MAN

I see you swagger
down 18th Street
bearing your
black felt hat
in hand
dreaming of buffalo
feasts and
pretty girls
with flashing
deep brown eyes

Hey Metis man
I bet you
didn't know
we watched you
with delight
knowing your
swagger was going
nowhere 'cause
it's Bingo night
tonight

I have come to have tremendous respect for the men of my culture. I know
the burdens they carry and the difficulty they experience in protecting their
families. It is not just the women who suffer. Our men have suffered from the
beginning of our history, and they have prevailed. We might criticize them,
but we know it has not been easy. They struggle with contradiction, abuse and
identity problems just as we women do. They carry our culture on their backs
in spite of being beaten in every way. They continue to work to support their
families. They still play with their children and jig with their women. They offer
us comfort when the world makes no sense. They are our strength, our pride and
our hope. Together we create and recreate our culture, our families and our future.

The future shines
bright and clear
when a Metis man
walks near.
He sings off tune
But it really
doesn't matter
'cause the song
comes from his heart.
I hear his belly laughter
And I also want to
sing.
When he taps his toes
my heart does
a jig.
he's a Metis man
and he needs to

know
his smile warms
our days and fills
our nights
It's having him
that makes our world
complete
Yup
There ain't no
man like a Metis man

Butterfly
I feel light like a butterfly
Why?
Because I am able to laugh
today
To sing
today
To live
today.

Imagine getting to the point of feeling free and light instead of carrying a burden so intense it's like waiting for your coffin to arrive. I lived like that most days. These days, however, I no longer sit in judgment on myself. I am not simply waiting for the coffin; I am pushing ahead, feeling a freedom I never thought possible. On a daily basis I run the gauntlet of feelings, but they no longer scare me. I understand where they are coming from and I do my best to appreciate how I feel. I no longer keep my secrets to myself. I share myself and in the process I am finding the most wonderful people coming into my life. This is not to say I will never feel overpowered; I just will not let the overpowering feelings crush me. And, I do not want to see the same crushing terrors in other Aboriginal women – terrors that I know rise from feelings of self-hatred, worthlessness and hopelessness. I know these feelings were fostered from a historical legacy of abuse. No woman should have to write in despair:

I am sick to death of being treated like I'm less than, or not enough. I feel like a failure. When I look in the mirror I see an ugly person, a person not dark enough for my Indian family and not light enough for my white family. No one wants me. I'm nothing. I see a fat bitch[34]

NOTES

27 When I was working on my Masters degree I had a professor who did not believe there was a place in philosophy for Native Philosophy. When I was on my PhD program I remember a graduate student who was fond of telling others that the only reason I was in the PhD program was because I was an Indian and not because I could do philosophy. I was humiliated when I heard a professor discussing me with other graduate students during a class break one day. He was ridiculing me for comparing Native philosophy to Eastern philosophy. They all turned and laughed as I walked back in the room.

28 While I understand that all students feel a measure of self-doubt, for me it was the direct result of thoughtless racist comments. I would drive myself crazy wondering if the student that said, "They have to graduate you. You are the first Native student in our department. They would be in trouble if you didn't make it," was simply being vindictive, or was she right. The racist comments by other students often left me doubting my own ability.

29 The hypocrisy that most offends me is when scholars ignore Native philosophies about the sacredness of land stewardship and tribal responsibility to land, yet applaud the excellent writing of people like Rachel Carson and David Henry Thoreau who also promoted environmental stewardship and social responsibility. I have seen scholars ignore Native accounts of the relationship between land and identity, then when one of their own kind writes about the importance of land to identity they applaud the writers' excellent ideas, and I wonder how they can ignore the fact that since contact with Europeans, Native Peoples have been talking about land and identity every chance they had.

30 Every day we confront the injustice of stereotypes in scholarly literature and are ignored or dismissed, every time we are told to cite the sources yet we know the sources to be distorted myths, we hurt. And every time we turn to non-native experts for source material we hurt. And every time we are told the words of our relatives or elders are not scholarly we hurt. And with each new hurt we continue to study and to write with the hope that someday we can undo these injustices. How much of ourselves we sacrifice can never be really explained.

31 Government, corporations and greed have all paved the way for the environmental problems we see today, and now in the midst of environmental activism accountability is called for. Ironically, the very people who held deeply religious views on the interconnectedness of all life are now confronted with hostility from animal-rights activists. The whaling issue in the United States between the Macaw people and animal-rights activists back in 1999 and the animal rights activists versus the Inuit in 1996 attest to how Aboriginal beliefs and practices are being dictated by non-Aboriginals.

32 Translation: All my relations

33 Aboriginal people did not write the books full of distorted stereotypes, but we must deal with them. Aboriginal people did not set out the requirements for degrees or for publishing, but we are confined by them. We can do our best to confront and change many of the stereotypes, we can work toward greater inclusivity in publishing, and we can even work toward degree requirements. With each, however, we must work diligently and carefully. Some areas can be attacked outright, but others may need negotiating and some may even need compromise, but we are in places now where Aboriginal people have a voice, and ultimately that voice will effect significant changes in education.

34 This comment was made on a test paper one day as the student struggled to acknowledge her fears. I prefer to keep her anonymity.

Lorraine Mayer

Bibliography

Aldama, Alturo. "Vision in the Four Directions: Five Hundred Years of Resistance and Beyond." In *As We Are Now: Mixedblood Essays on Race and Identity.* Berkeley, California: University of California Press, 1997.

Anderson, Kim. *Recognition of Being: Reconstructing Native Womanhood.* Toronto: Second Story Press, 2000.

Arteago, Alfred. "An Other Tongue." In A. Arteago (ed.) *An Other Tongue: Nation and Ethnicity in the Borderlands.* Durham & London: Duke University Press, 1994.

Cummins, Bryon D., John L. Steckley. *Aboriginal Policing: A Canadian Perspective.* Toronto: Prentice Hall, 2003.

Flanagan, Thomas. "The Case Against Metis Aboriginal Rights." Canadian Public Policy, Vol. 9, No. 3 (Sept. 1983): 314-325.

Green, Joyce. "Missing Women." Canadian Dimension, Sept. 2004.

Hunter, Anna. "The Violence that Indigenous Women Face." Canadian Dimension, March/April 2005.

Lugones, Maria. "On Complex Communications." Hypatia 21:3 (2006): 75-85

Morrison, Sheila Jones. *Rotten to the Core: The Politics of the Manitoba Metis Federation.* Victoria, B.C., 1995.

Racine, Darrell, Dale Lakevold. *Misty Lake.* Lake Audy, Manitoba: Adler & Ringe, 2000.

Spencer, Rainier. "Race and Mixed Race A Personal Tour in *As We Are Now: Mixedblood Essays on Race and Identity.* Berkeley, California: University of California Press, 1997.

Penn, William S. *As We Are Now: Mixedblood Essays on Race and Identity.* Berkeley, California: University of California Press, 1997.

Zack, Naomi. *Thinking About Race.* Belmont, California: Wadsworth, 1998.

Zack, Naomi. Ed *American Mixed Race: The Culture of Microdiversity.* Lanham, Maryland: Rowman & Littlefield, 1995, *p. xvii.*